PENGUIN BOOKS

The God Boy

Ian Cross has spent much of his career as a journalist. He edited the *New Zealand Listener* from 1973 to 1977 when he became chairman of the Broadcasting Corporation of New Zealand. *The God Boy* was first published in 1957 and was followed by *The Backward Sex* (1960), *After Anzac Day* (1961) and *The Family Man* (1993). He has also written his autobiography, *The Unlikely Bureaucrat* (1988).

Roger Robinson, Senior Professor of English at Victoria University of Wellington, New Zealand, was co-editor of the *Oxford Companion to New Zealand Literature* (1998). His most recent book is *Robert Louis Stevenson: His Best Pacific Writings* (2002).

D0785126

THE GOD BOY

Ian Cross

PENGUIN BOOKS

PENGUIN BOOKS

Published by the Penguin Group
Penguin Books Ltd, 80 Strand, London WC2R 0RL, England
Penguin Putnam Inc., 375 Hudson Street, New York, New York 10014, USA
Penguin Books Australia Ltd, 250 Camberwell Road,
Camberwell, Victoria 3124, Australia
Penguin Books Canada Ltd, 10 Alcorn Avenue, Toronto,
Ontario, Canada M4V 3B2
Penguin Books India (P) Ltd, 11 Community Centre,
Panchsheel Park, New Delhi – 110 017, India
Penguin Books (NZ) Ltd, Cnr Rosedale and Airborne Roads,
Albany, Auckland, New Zealand
Penguin Books (South Africa) (Pty) Ltd, 24 Sturdee Avenue,
Rosebank 2196, South Africa

Penguin Books Ltd, Registered Offices: 80 Strand, London WC2R 0RL, England

www.penguin.com

First published in 1957 by Harcourt, Brace and Co., New York
Published in Penguin Books 1962
Reprinted with new introduction in Penguin Classics 2003

1

Printed in England by Clays Ltd, St Ives plc

INTRODUCTION

The God Boy is a deceptively modest masterpiece. It purports to be the story of a mere boy. It limits its language to his gauche thirteen-year-old's idiom, and its viewpoint to his eager naïvety and inexperience. Its setting is a small provincial town at the world's most insignificant margin. Its scope, it seems to insist, is domestic. The school and the town wharf are its most exotic locations, and a whiskery dropout who fishes all day its most unconventional character. In New Zealand, the first page affirms, 'we don't actually get wars and gangster fights', so this is not, in 1957, to be a novel of Cold War anxiety or social conflict. Nor is its home-loving, prepubescent, Catholic central character much of a 1950s teenage rebel. There is neither sexual nor social radicalism in *The God Boy*. Its scale seems much smaller.

Yet by the end of Jimmy Sullivan's stumbling, half-comprehended story, the reader has encountered murder, trauma and tragedy, witnessed the warping of a promising mind and the destruction of a family. We have seen the cruelty beneath society's surface. We have confronted, if that is our belief, mortal sin. We have come to doubt the existence of order or meaning in human affairs. We question the moral decency and compassion of God. The scale of this book is larger than it pretends.

From the first page, these multiple levels are in process, and the reader is involved in the narration as an active participant. Jimmy's boyish voice and limited language impel us immediately (from the first sentence there is scarcely an exaggeration) to perceive what lies beneath his self-deluding postures. When he says he doesn't care, we already know he does. When he claims he likes to remember whatever it is he is going to tell us, we already know he can't help himself. When he strikes his pose of teenage warrior braggadocio – 'I know I would love shooting and kicking out at my enemies' – we see how sensitive and hurt he is, and understand that some personal damage is impelling him to violence ('kicking out' is the giveaway). Already we pity him, though we also see the danger that he might move on to behaviour beyond the pale of our pity. For an opening page in which a boy narrator just talks about going to the dentist, that is a complex and important range of responses.

The complexity is sustained and rewarding. Ian Cross's narrative craft never falters as he builds the many-layered text on its simple base. Jimmy Sullivan at thirteen is a homeless adolescent in the care of a Catholic boarding school. The action, he tells us, is mainly from two years earlier, three days of misunderstanding and ill will that ended his parents' marriage and (we understand from the telling) his peace of mind and emotional stability.

The text is thus an interplay between three levels of observation and interpretation. There is Jimmy at eleven, childishly observant, impulsive and anxious, as excited about his new bike as his family's strife. There is Jimmy at thirteen, defensive, brash, competitive, clearly disturbed for all his pose of indifference and resilience. And there is the reader, adroitly enabled to see around and through the child's uncomprehending consciousness, and to bring adult judgement to the drama.

We understand far more than Jimmy about his complex relationship with his sister, and her more knowing reaction to their parents' crisis. We recognize the early stirrings of his sexuality. We assess the interventions and the intentions of the priest, nuns, neighbours, police and social workers. We hear much more of his parents' hatred and its causes than he does. As Jimmy half reluctantly describes their 'trouble', 'nagging away at each other', 'big rows', 'a lot of talk like that I can just about repeat word for word', we soon know that we are witnessing a domestic tragedy of resentment, anger, drunkenness, vituperation, womanizing, claustrophobia, illicit abortion and finally murder.

These serious moral matters never make the novel heavy going. With Jimmy's youthful enthusiasms and irreverence, his unpredictable thought associations and zestful curiosity, the narration is always vital and engaging and often comic. The episode in Chapter 4 where he pesters the overweight abortionist (as we quickly recognize her to be) with inquiries about her bulk is very funny, even while we see and dislike her ill temper and mean spirit. That dialogue worked brilliantly in the film and stage versions of the story.

Ian Cross, thirty-two when this first novel was published in 1957, was already a successful journalist. Chief reporter with the Wellington *Dominion*, he had been awarded an associate fellowship in journalism (despite having no prior university education) at Harvard University in 1954–5. His reporting skill gives the extra edge in the novel of a child's fresh particularity of observation and Jimmy's loyal enthusiasm for his own small world. Raggleton is made credible and familiar, even to the reader with no knowledge of 1950s provincial New Zealand. The wooden houses, the few shops with their rusting corrugated-iron verandas, 'two or three cars parked in the main street', the war memorial on the corner, the hill behind the school, the 'metal' (grit and sand) roads outside the centre, the scruffy wharf and beach of rolling surf backed by sand dunes straggly with lupin, where the 'big boys and girls [lie] slopping over each other' – it is all constructed in deft detail and (very skilfully) made to assume those larger proportions we all recall from our childhood.

The ordinariness and familiarity of the location and its community, and the affection we quickly form for Jimmy himself, make it more disturbing when his inner anxieties break out into violence. The literature of teenage turmoil has few scenes as painful as Jimmy throwing stones at his friend Bloody Jack (Chapter 15). That whole section of his petty rampage, and the later one of his breakdown and self-inflicted scalding, draw their power from the counterpoint between Jimmy's near-delirious mental state and behaviour and the childish honesty and lack of self-knowledge with which he describes what happens. Equally painful to read are the rituals and mantras he calls his 'protection tricks', trying pathetically to shut out the sound and significance of his parents' quarrels. The boy talks of running the hot water and choosing a song as innocently as he might describe football practice, while we see only too clearly the psychological wounds being inflicted. The shortcomings of the narration ingeniously

7

impel us to be participants more than observers. The novel's imaginative force comes not only from witnessing the dark clenching of a bright and open young mind, but also from the experience of actually inhabiting a consciousness even as it becomes crippled.

Within his psychological decline lies a deeper spiritual dimension. Remarkably, in Jimmy's sadly perky chatter, Cross has found a fresh and vivid way to put into fiction some of the world's most fundamental questions of ethics, metaphysics and theology. The title comes from Jimmy's conscientious yet fresh-minded struggle to comprehend his situation in the religious terms he has been taught. It is not necessary to be a Christian to see the pertinence of the issues. Cross himself was no longer a Catholic at the time of writing, though he retained from his schooling, he has said, a sense 'that good and evil exist' and 'a complete acceptance of the doctrine of original sin . . . it's the only doctrine that . . . makes it possible for you to live with the conflicting elements of human beings – the element of baseness as against the element of virtue'.

Virtue and baseness can be seen in conflict within Cross's little protagonist. Even while he questions God's intentions and conduct in permitting his undeserved suffering, he still retains an utterly literal belief in God's presence and authority. Hence Jimmy can tell Sister Angela, 'I'm a God boy, Sister. You don't have to worry about me.' He has no doubt at that point (Chapter 13) that he is 'right in there with her on God's side'. The teaching nun, as Jimmy puts it, 'was inclined to be on the lookout for the Devil', and is proved right, as 'the element of baseness' increasingly asserts itself in him over 'the element of virtue'.

The schoolboy idiom remains naïve, endearing and funny, but the theological questions become increasingly radical: 'if [God] is such a hot scone why doesn't he do more of the day-to-day stuff?' 'it was as much God's fault as mine, if not more, because I had done my best and he hadn't done a damn thing'. By the end, he has lost his confidence that he is on God's team: 'Protestants were off side with God, and so was I.' And his God has changed from being a dilatory team captain into a calculating antagonist to be distrusted and opposed: 'I don't care what else God is going to try on me, but whatever it is, he had better watch his step.' In terms

8

of moral equity he has good grounds for complaint. 'I get annoyed at God for putting one across on me the way he did . . . I certainly didn't do any big wrong. That's what I have against God. Me so little and he God.' So his impulse to 'kick out' turns finally on God, too, and 'once or twice I have . . . bitten the wafer right through with my teeth to try to hurt him'.

The book ends with what seems an affirmation of Jimmy's strength. The first edition carried a dust-jacket reassurance that Jimmy's 'feud with God is evidence of a stubborn sense of good, which will ensure his survival'. Today the novel's last sentence seems more ambiguous. '[T]his good memory of mine', which keeps Jimmy awake at night reliving his trauma, may as he says be proof that 'nothing will ever really get me down'. Or it may prove that the random cruelty of life already has.

An early journalistic job in the middle of a civil war in Panama had given Ian Cross a lasting sense of 'the chaos and disorder of life around us', and an impulse to write fiction that 'tries to give it a meaning; and to that extent I'm only partly a fiction writer; I'm more a striver after an explanation'. His later novels continued the effort. *The Backward Sex* (1960) focused on the psychological disorder of nascent sexuality, with the narrator this time seventeen and, like Jimmy, forthright and credible yet revealing much more to the reader than he understands himself. *After Anzac Day* (1961) sought meaning through the interaction of multiple viewpoints, the various occupants of a Wellington home reacting to life and each other in utterly diverse ways. After a long hiatus, Cross returned to fiction with *The Family Man* (1993), a historical retrospect on New Zealand in the later twentieth century, partly auto-biographical, and another *tour de force* where the narrator's limitations, like Jimmy's, generate intensity and pathos.

Cross's absence from fiction for thirty years was due not to any decline in his creative energy but to its diversion into the senior positions he held in business, journalism and public service. In the mid-1970s he was a notably successful editor of the *New Zealand Listener* at a time when the weekly was a major force in the country's cultural and intellectual life. He went on to be chairman of the then New Zealand Broadcasting Corporation through the period of television's most explosive growth, and for several years held the line for public broadcasting against encroaching commercialism. In between, he has been successful as a media analyst, always affirming the responsibility of the contemporary media to 'hold up . . . higher standards of expression and a wider range of creative exploration'.

The God Boy is sometimes compared with *The Catcher in the Rye* (1951). Like J. D. Salinger, or Henry James in *What Maisie Knew* (1897), or Alan Sillitoe in 'The Loneliness of the Long Distance Runner' (1959), Cross has made an immature central figure tragically significant without being patronizing or sentimental. His novel is often cited in New Zealand as an instance of the national literature's special skill with child observers or narrators, a tradition established (it is said) in Katherine Mansfield's stories. It may be more helpful to consider Cross alongside one of his best New Zealand contemporaries, M. K. Joseph, whose war novels (notably *A Soldier's Tale*, 1976) take a special force from what might be called the typically semi-detached New Zealand viewpoint. New Zealand's geographical remoteness and small population perhaps give it a way of looking at portentous events (whether European war or marital murder) from an observant, partly involved, but partly detached perspective. But sometimes the small observer gets hurt.

A major influence was Mark Twain. Cross has said that *Huckleberry Finn* (1884) 'released writers and readers from the bondage of colonial belief that literature was governed by a special language'. The unliterary schoolboy idiom of *The God Boy*, though elements of English and American slang are evident, is as distinctively New Zealand as Huck Finn's or Holden Caulfield's are American. A car is 'a long black job', his rival Legs falls off his bike 'in a beautiful gutzer' and he assures the reader that 'blowing my top this day should not be taken as a smack at Father Gilligan'. Such limited expressive range reflects the national linguistic temperament as well as Jimmy's youth. It is a limitation that enables Cross, with the reader's participation, to load increasing emotional force into banal words and phrases like 'iffey', 'blowing my top', or 'I didn't give a darn.'

10

Cross said that Twain 'was making a declaration of independence for New World writing . . . [to] celebrate . . . our own voices'. In the very different world of twenty-first century global literature in English, it is hard to remember what a radical departure this still was in 1957, and how significant books like *The God Boy* (published first in New York, then in 1958 in London) have been in preparing the way for Achebe, Atwood, Coetzee, Hulme, Malouf, Rushdie and others.

A useful comparison from Cross's own decade is Graham Greene, another journalist-novelist given to exploring good and evil. In *The End of the Affair* (1951), Sarah Miles communicates with God in her journal with a personal and almost critical directness of voice not unlike Jimmy Sullivan's, and not much less naïve. In narrative craft, moral insight and imaginative force, *The God Boy* stands up well in such company.

Ian Cross wrote a stage adaptation of *The God Boy* that was successfully performed in New Zealand in 1999. The novel has been filmed for television, and there is an opera version, with libretto by Jeremy Commons. Well established as an excellent text for school and university study, the book has become a live element in New Zealand's national culture. Its more universal relevance and literary accomplishment are self-evident. *The God Boy* seems likely to remain a moving and challenging novel, so long as children suffer from their parents' conflicts, and there are readers to appreciate the fine art of first-person narrative.

Roger Robinson, 2003

Note:

This introduction draws on Ian Cross's memoir of his public service years, *The Unlikely Bureaucrat* (1988); on his paper 'The God Boy', originally delivered in 1962, published in *Journal of New Zealand Literature* 8 (1990); and on interviews in *Directions*, (1995), ed. Neville Glasgow, and the *New Zealand Listener*, 1 August 1987.

I

You would think I care, and I did for a while, but not now. While it was happening, and for some time after, I cared so much I must have been nearly mad, but I don't care now. I don't. I can remember everything though; it is not that I don't care because I have forgotten. Boy, I can remember every second, just about, and I will lie in bed at night and think about it, because I can't help myself, and I sort of like to do it, but I don't care.

I suppose my attitude to the whole affair is like going to a dentist, at least the way I feel when I go to a dentist. All nervous and worried and scared, but once I'm in the chair and the drill has been boring away for a while, it makes no difference to me: I just sit there and I think that if the dentist started to cut me up into little pieces I wouldn't care. I'm like some of these soldiers that get medals and these gangsters in the films. It seems silly for me to say this, with me living in a place like this, and all the nuns flapping around, prayers and church and confession and communion, and all that stupid stuff. It seems silly, as I say, for a kid like me here saying I feel that way, but I know how I would be in a war or a gangster fight. It's a pity that, in a country like New Zealand, we don't actually get wars and gangster fights, and I know that you have to go halfway around the world to find that kind of rough stuff. If you go one way you hit the South Pole, so that's no use, and the other way, you have to keep on going over the sea until you're way past Australia before any decent trouble begins. But even so, allowing that it may seem silly for a kid like me saying I feel this way, I know how I would be in a war or gangster fight. I know it, just know it. I know I don't give a darn what ever happens to me, and I know I would love shooting and kicking out at my enemies, not giving a darn what they try to do to me.

Even now, and I'm still thirteen, I'm good enough to be boss of the kids here, and some of them are nearly fifteen. When I get into a scrap I fight to the end, and anybody would have to kill me before I'd stop going for them. They'd have to kill me or give in, because there's nothing they can do to me to stop me getting at them unless they kill me. Ray Brown, for instance. He beat me and beat me, because he is stronger, but he is soft, and when he saw all the blood over my face he wanted to stop, really, though he went on fighting. He still hit at me, but he wanted to stop, and he started to get frightened because I was still after him, not giving a darn, even though I had hardly been able to touch him and yet had been messed up myself. When he started to want to stop, even though he went on fighting, I got him by the cheeks with each hand and just tore at them. Then he got really frightened and I made a bigger mess of him than he made of me. I'm not a skite, but if I was fighting a man it would be the same. He would have to kill me to beat me. Knocking me out wouldn't do him any good because when I came to I would go after him again, no matter how many times he knocked me out. I would go after him for weeks and months till he either gave in or killed me. And I wouldn't give a darn. It wouldn't be any use breaking my arms or legs or anything like that; I would still go after him.

As I said, I'm boss round here and there's no arguments, really. I keep in with the nuns all right, too, because I'm pretty good with my prayers and the other stuff, and though there was a tremendous fuss about that big fight with Ray Brown, that was a year ago and all forgotten. I keep in with the prayers because you have to, and me with no home now, I need this place, for the education and all that. You have to be educated, and I like learning. For that matter, though I said all this prayer and communion and confession is stupid, I don't mind it, really. You can't be smart all the time. I'm very smart, too, by the way. Top of the class, and

I can see the nuns are impressed by me. I've always been very clever. But I was talking about religion. Boy, I'm clever enough to have my own ideas there. You know, if I went after God I could beat him, too, unless he killed me. And he wouldn't want to, if I know God, and there I would have him. I'd be Pope, whether he liked it or not, and boy, I would tell people about God, and he wouldn't be able to do anything about it, except kill me.

It doesn't worry me the slightest bit talking about my mother and father, because I don't care. But I'll tell you how I used to care just to show you. I was eleven then. I'll try and get everything into order, make a story out of it sort of, so you can see. I don't mind talking, though I never have before, because I know I don't care, and I don't mind thinking it, and I'm glad to talk, especially as I don't care.

I remember walking home with Dad that time and he saying, 'Home we go to our loving wife and mother and one more round in the heavyweight championship of the world.' I knew what he meant but I said nothing and he went on. 'You don't like my drinking, boy. That's it, isn't it?'

Funny, that was just after the bike business, now that I think of it. Joe Waters and I had been fooling around with his bike this evening when we saw Dad coming up the road, on his way home from work. Dad was quite good-looking, well-built, you know, but not big. Mum was bigger than he was. And he had this lame arm, and when he was walking quickly it jiggled at his side. It was jiggling this day. Our town, you know that place, Raggleton, way down there by the sea, was a big place, no village in the country. It had a hotel two stories high, and two barbershops, and there were pictures twice a week. There must be well over a thousand people living there. Dad worked in the harbour board office, and once he said to me:

'I haven't been a success in life, son.'

'You certainly are better than a lot of people round here, Dad,' I said. 'You dress up for work every day, for instance, and a lot of others don't.'

He never saw the point of that, and now I see really he was talking about something else. When you think of what happened, whatever it was, it was not a success, though I don't care. I'm just as well off.

This bike. We were playing with that as Dad came up the road. I didn't have a bike and always wanted one, so I took the bike off Joe and we worked this stunt with me pedalling fast down toward Joe, taking my feet off the pedals and putting my hands on the seat, and with a shove jumping back off the bike, landing on my feet more or less. Joe caught the bike.

These were the times I did care, so don't get confused when I talk about my feelings then and confuse them with my feelings now. I'm just remembering my own feelings when I talk this way, like you can remember anything else.

Well, my feelings then were pretty good, I know, because they got so bad when Dad spoke. He was right up to us when I had finished working that stunt.

'You're really red-hot, son.'

I knew as soon as I heard his voice. I felt bad. I didn't like to think of him and Mum at all, because I knew what would happen when we got home. I knew all right.

Joe Waters pulled the bike round and said, 'I'll be off home now. See you in the morning, Jimmy. Good-bye, Mr Sullivan.'

Dad took a step toward Joe and said, 'Let me show you something there.' There was a smile on his face that was loose and didn't look as though it was for anything in particular. When he had been drinking and was in a good mood he smiled like that, sometimes sitting, just sitting, in the big armchair in the lounge at home. He wasn't as big as most other men, and not as wide, and in the big armchair, sitting there smiling at nothing, he looked really little. Standing over Joe, he looked big.

I rushed over and said:

'Dad, it's time we went home.'

'How did you know what your old father was going to do?' he asked.

Well, I knew he was going to ride the bike and make a fool of himself, and as he looked at me he must have seen what I was worrying about because he smiled and said, 'You're right, son. Let's get on home.'

As he walked home he made those remarks about 'home to our loving wife and mother' and then asked me if his drinking worried me. That's where I really meant to begin the story, but I got mixed up there, interested in the bike. I've grown out of liking bikes, don't you worry. They are useful, I know, but I certainly don't like them much. Anyway, there I lost the story, which should have started off with Dad drunk and our going straight home after that. But now that I have mentioned Joe Waters, I'll just say this about him. You know his mother and father used to go to church together with him, and once a month they'd take him to the pictures. I used to think that was great, and I couldn't help envying Joe. When I look back I've got a lot of ideas about parents, and you might think that is funny, me with my background, and not really caring, but I have these ideas, and I think they could be described as scientific.

Heck now, I started off with Dad talking to me as we walked home, and here we are no further on. Well, I didn't say a word when he asked me about his drinking, and he went on:

'I've been looking at your face, Jimmy, and I know you don't like me drinking. But mark my words, when you grow up, you'll probably find that all the decency in life you can find is in a bar, drinking with a few friends, real friends.'

I was thinking about what would happen when we got home, and what it would be like. It's taking me as long to get Dad and I home as it would for me to be actually going home myself in those days. I can remember, before all the trouble began, running up the road to home. Later on all I wanted to do was run down that road. You've got to remember I wasn't so old then, and felt these things.

17

Well, anyway, Dad and I got home and I went inside ahead of him, and, of course, it happened to me again.

I went inside and, you know, even though all this had been going on for a long time now I still half expected that I would come home one day and it would be all over and everything right again. Even then I remember going inside and there was this hope. A kid is always hoping. That is where they are different from grownups. When a kid hopes he really hopes, but when a grownup hopes, I get the idea he hopes and doesn't hope at the same time. My going inside then. I suppose it was the warmth of the house and seeing Mum, bending over the stove cooking, looking so big and warm herself, that made me hope.

'We're home,' I said as we went in the kitchen.

'Wash your hands and come to the table,' she said, without looking up. That would be because Dad was behind me.

'Be just a sec, Mum,' I said. 'Be back to eat a horse.'

I ducked back past Dad into the passage and closed the door behind me.

'Put the towel back on the rack, young man. Don't throw it over the edge of the bath.'

She was always on to me about that.

After I closed the door I really wanted to go on down the passage to the bathroom. I wanted to, yet I didn't. I had to listen. It was funny with me. I couldn't help listening to what my mother and father were saying to each other, even though it did me no good. This time I knew what they would say, and I knew what would happen to me, and still I listened. I moved a little up from the door into the middle of the passage and stretched both my arms out till my fingers were touching the wallpaper on each side. I was a queer fish, I suppose, but that was the way I was. That wallpaper, touching it like that, was one of my protection tricks. I still like wallpaper, if you want to know, wallpaper with those whirling designs as a pattern.

I heard my mother say, 'You drunken pig,' to my father.

'You go about with the boy while you are sodden with drink.'

'For God's sake shut up,' he said.

'You ought to be ashamed of yourself.'

'Dish up the food and keep your nagging tongue in your head.'

A lot of talk like that I can just about repeat word for word. I have a very good memory, there is no doubt about that.

When I heard those words it happened to me again. This must have been the fourth or fifth time I had to use my protection tricks. As I heard them talking like that I could see how mother would be looking because I had seen her that way often with my father. She would be all hot and warm, and she'd stare at him in a way that would frighten me, and she always had a fist up alongside her head. Even though I was out in the passage I could feel her so much it was almost as though she was pressed up right next to me. I pushed my fingers till my nails dug into the wallpaper, and, as I said, it happened to me again.

The air just went cold, as it did those times before, and started sticking to my skin, on my arms and legs and face, everywhere. I had seen a marble statue in a museum, a well-built man doubled over throwing something, and the feeling reminded me of him. It was as if I was starting to be made of marble. And my heart started banging away so much it shook me. I knew what to do and I managed to get to the bathroom, though I could hardly move my legs. I said, 'Hail Mary, full of grace, the Lord is with you, blessed art thou amongst women and blessed is the fruit of thy womb, Jesus,' and turned on the hot-water tap over the bath, and shoved my hands under. The hot water cleaned away the marble feeling wherever it touched and there was only the ordinary skin there. Then I said, 'Holy Mary, Mother of God, pray for us sinners, now and at the hour of our death, amen,' and dipped the flannel in the hot water and rubbed it all over me. I got wet and messed up, yet it worked. The

19

last protection trick of mine was to sing, 'Jingle-bells, jingle bells, jingle all the way, oh what fun, it is to ride in a one-horse open sleigh'. I had other songs, 'Hail Queen of the Sea', which the nuns taught us at school, 'It's a Long Way to Tipperary', which my father taught me, and, naturally, the national anthem. I only had to sing one song at these times. It didn't make any difference which one.

2

I KNOW the difference between men and women, of course. Men have the whatnots down below but women haven't; on the other hand, women blow out up top but men don't. Men and women can get married and have babies if they want to, although Joe Waters used to argue that it was possible to be married without having babies, and that was what he was going to do. It wasn't that Joe didn't like babies, by the way; he didn't like what everybody said you had to do to get them. He reckoned he saw a man and a woman in the lupines down at the beach doing it, thinking that no one was around, and that it looked the silliest business in the world, unless you counted going down under the sea in a submarine. Joe always had a bee in his bonnet about submarines, too, for some reason, although he had never actually seen one.

I mention this about men and women to show that I know what I'm talking about. With Mum and Dad now, they must have got married and had their children—there are two of us, by the way; I have a big sister named Molly—they must have had their children and changed their minds, and then it was too late. Why they changed their minds I don't know, because both of them seemed all right. Mum was very bad-tempered and quiet toward the end, and Dad always did drink too much, but besides that they were all right to me, at least when they were not together—then, of course, everything seemed to come out of joint. Even when they didn't have big rows, they'd always be nagging away at each other. Sometimes when there didn't seem the need to, as, for instance, when Dad said at the tea-table, 'Bert and his wife are having a bit of a do over at their place on Saturday night. I don't suppose you want to go, eh?'

'For goodness sake, no,' said Mum.

'I knew you would take it like that. Here I am stuck in this godforsaken dump and getting no fun out of life and you won't even come out and help. Come on, eh; you can sit in a corner and glare at me the way you always do, that won't matter.'

'You don't usually find it necessary to even bother with me.'

'Too right I don't. If you must know, Bert's wife was in the office and she asked. It's a husband and wife affair, so I can't go without you.'

'I'm past being humiliated by you in public, having to watch your drunken foolishness and everybody looking on.'

'That's your evil mind, you know. You're heading for the rat house, the way you talk. Imagining things. I'm a very popular man, plenty of friends, and I can move in any circle and I'm always a perfect gentleman. I'd have plenty of friends if it wasn't for you. And you talk about being humiliated by me. People think you are queer, that's what people think about you.'

That's the way they went on ever since I could remember. Yet by themselves they were fine. Dad would help me fly kites and talk away to me, and Mum was really great. Somehow I don't really blame them; I blame God.

I have got a lot of ideas about God. I pray as much as anybody, even though I am tough, yet I'm not too sure I like God. It seems to me that if he is what they say he is he has a very funny way of showing it. That's what gets me annoyed sometimes, and then I give him a piece of my mind. I don't go in for this soft soap all the time. I tell him what I think because he darn well knows it, anyway. I'll be praying, you know, as we all have to before class each morning, with the nuns, and when I'm feeling anything but mealy-mouthed I let him know.

'Our Father, who art in heaven, you give me a pain in the neck,' I'll say.

It is just a feeling, and, of course, I apologize usually

22

when I feel better, yet there is no hiding the fact that in some ways I am dissatisfied with God. There is an expression I read in a book that I shouldn't have been reading (I read everything I can get my hands on, though), and I like the way it sums my feelings up. The thin end of the purse, that's it. Looking back I can't help thinking that I got the thin end of the purse—that's a boxing expression, by the way—and this from God, and me only little. He could have waited till I got bigger. Even now it wouldn't be so bad, as I am in a better position. I should think that God should wait till children are over twelve at least before he starts swinging Sunday punches. That's another boxing expression. That's why I get annoyed with him, and occasionally I think that I will go after him. If enough people started a mutiny, not against the Church, mind you, but against God, maybe he will sit up and take notice. I've always been interested in God.

Don't mistake me about myself, though. A lot of good things happened to me and they are what God could use in his defence. Raggleton was a nice place, down there by the sea which roared quietly into your ear all the time, like a cat purring. All my life till I was taken away from there I could stop at any time of the day and cock my head and hear that purring. And at night laying in bed it was extra plain, blur-blur-blurring away, and that was the sound of the whole world. A kid in a place by the sea is lucky that way, being able to hear what is going on in the whole world. Not living by the sea is just the same as living underground and not being able to see the sky. The sea is just as important as the sky, and now I often want to hear it and yet I cannot except from memory.

We had a sermon once at church and the priest said hell was like an ocean of fire. He was talking through his hat, going on like that, about every wave being red-hot. Hell and the sea don't go together and that is that.

And there are lots of nice people by the sea. I used to sit and watch Bloody Jack for hours on the wharf. He'd sit there talking all the time, to me when I was there and the fish when I wasn't. He would be fishing, you understand, dirty and old and knobbly. He never shaved, yet he never really had a beard, half his face being covered by a black fuzzy mess that never grew into anything one way or the other. And he'd natter away all the time, and never catch many fish, mainly because he couldn't be bothered replacing his bait when he lost it. I don't know why we called him Bloody Jack.

Sitting there on the wharf, in those old clothes, near where the freezing works discharged the old blood and guts (you could smell it as well as see it in the water), and the sea way on out there over the bar, he was a big friend of mine.

'Young'un,' he'd say, 'a man might as well fish all the time and be done with it, especially if you've got a pension, because that's what we are all doing anyway.'

He'd go on like that, getting really involved way over my head, about everybody was fishing for something, that being life. He was not all there upstairs, I suppose, yet the way he talked on and on in a growl was good. He could make noises with his stomach, too, that were really amazing. Real control he had. Some days he would wriggle his stomach so that you could hear it a mile off. I would laugh at that, and as a special show he would finish a demonstration with a blowoff that you wouldn't believe was possible, you really wouldn't, it was so long and loud. He never would belch, though.

'All expulsions of air should be from the lower bowel, boy', he said. 'Don't forget that and you will never have a minute's trouble with your digestion.'

And then there were the regular fishermen who would drop into Raggleton sometimes. They would always let you look over their boats, and tell you about sharks and whales and octopuses. I've actually seen dead sharks and octopuses. All those men were friendly and tough and us boys respected them very much. The big man was Mike Venutti, who had two boats, and he would tell us about Italy, and he could sing like nobody's business, down there in the sun. It would be sissy for anybody else to sing like he did.

Raggleton had this port, and the wharf, and the freezing works, which had a railway line running into the middle of it practically. And around the bend of the bay, behind the port and the town, everybody lived. The coast took a big curve there, and right back of the town was the sea again, hitting a big beach. A peninsula is the correct name for the place, and the county is actually called Peninsula County. So kids had the sea and the sand, and rocks under the cliffs at one end of the beach, where crabs and other shelly fishes lived, as well as the normal things that kids have in living in a town. So I was lucky there.

I bet our beach was the best place in the world for kids. The sea itself, there, was no place for sissies, as the breakers came in like rows of steam-rollers and would flatten you if you didn't dive under or go with them. There was a long stretch of sand right down to the mole at the harbour entrance on one side and right up to the cliffs on the other. Behind there were great sand hills covered with lupine and marram grass with a few pohutukawa trees here and there. There was actually a track through the lupines and around one of the hills that came out near the back of our place, so it was only a few minutes for me to get down to the beach. All the kids of Raggleton would play there because there was no limit to what you could do. For that matter, a lot of grownups used to mess around there, too, especially the big boys and girls. Often during the summer we kids would come across them laying around under the lupines slopping over each other.

One Sunday afternoon my mother came out walking with me, I don't know why, and without actually telling her why, I got her to go down to the wharf, and as I knew he would be, old Bloody Jack was there, sitting alone and growling away as he spoke to the fish. I've heard him talking about books to fish.

'Look who's with me,' I called out that day as we got near Jack.

He turned around and looked, hardly glancing at me, but staring at my mother. There was nothing special that day about her. She had an ordinary dress on, the spotted one with dots, I think, yet he stared at her a long time, then grunted, and said nothing. He didn't say another word while we were there. It was remarkable, that; it was the only time I ever heard him not talking. We were only there a minute or so, because my mother wasn't very interested in where we were, and certainly didn't seem interested in Jack, and then she complained about the smell, so we went back up. I looked over my shoulder, and it wasn't till we were a fair way off that I could hear Jack starting to talk again.

I tried to talk to my mother about Jack and she didn't listen, so I gave up. I don't think she even knew I was interested in him, really. Jack never said anything to me about her coming down that day, and I never said anything to him, either. With Mum not saying anything, it was a queer business all around.

3

AFTER that evening when I came home with Dad, and he
and Mum started fighting, it was all over in three days. My
good memory often kicks over like a motor bike that is
starting—bang, and there is Dad walking up the road that
time Joe and I were fooling with his bike; bang again, it
is Monday morning, the engine is really started roaring
away in my head until it is all over.

I got up Monday morning at my usual time, about seven-
thirty, and could hear Dad moving around upstairs, his feet
like bumps on the ceiling of my bedroom. Our house was
an old two-storey one, and I had the bedroom downstairs.
It was a funny place for a bedroom, and originally wasn't
meant for that purpose at all, I believe, but I didn't mind.
I actually liked it there; you could hear the noises of the
house and the sea better there than anywhere else. Dad and
Mum slept upstairs, and so did Molly, though she was away
at school then, of course.

Everything was a little old, except that furniture in the
lounge. The wallpaper, the big brass vase on the wooden
stand at the end of the passage, the high ceilings that were
stained in a few of the rooms, the worn carpet on the stairs,
with the banisters shaky in one part, and the floor in the
kitchen that creaked when you stood near the window. It
was really a great place, and the few times any kids from
school came home with me, they thought it was wonderful,
too. These new houses they build now, they're nothing. I'd
have liked to have brought some of the kids home often
except that I was worried about something going wrong.
Like that time I came home and Mum was sick, not letting
me upstairs. Later on I heard Dad actually blaming her for
being sick. That must have been the first time I felt queer.

27

Our house had very high ceilings, because it had been built so long ago; I suppose the floors were high, too. I mean the whole place was jacked up a long way off the ground before it even started. There was a front entrance which nobody ever used, I don't know why, and a side entrance, and at both of them you had to walk up eight concrete steps to get level with the ground floor. The side entrance took you through the back porch, which led to the passage that ran right through the house.

I used to be able to hit each room off the passage dead on the nose with my eyes closed; three steps to the bathroom door on the left, eight to the kitchen on the right, five to the lounge on the left, six more to the foot of the stairs on the right, and twelve to near the end on the left to my bedroom. When I was about six I was practising touching the door-knobs with my eyes closed—at the stairs I just tapped the bottom step—when Molly sneaked into my bedroom and jumped out as I was putting my hand out there, giving an awful scream which actually made me wet my pants a little bit, though I never gave the show away.

Anyway, this morning I heard Dad upstairs when I got up, and we had breakfast together. Though both Mum and Dad were silent, I felt much better, and as I was cleaning my teeth afterwards I thought that really I would be as happy as anybody else if I had a bike, no matter what was going on between my parents. I was cleaning my teeth in the bathroom, of course; that was where I got most of my bright ideas, although I am certainly not saying that my bike was one of them. That was the worst idea I ever had, as it turned out. If I had thought of the bike anywhere else but the bathroom I might not have done anything about it. But the bathroom was an especial place because of the black paint somebody had put on the walls. It was really great. Joe Waters and some of the other kids went to the lavatory there one time they were playing in our back yard and it was a big kick for me to hear them say that even the governor-general wouldn't have black walls to his bathroom.

Dad said one of the other tenants before us must have been a maniac. Anyway, all the walls were painted this deep dark colour that made the washbasin, the lavatory bowl, and the bath itself look so darned white, and with the red linoleum that Mum put down on the floor the whole place was pretty interesting on the whole. The bath was one of those jobs that stood on legs that looked as though they might have come off a bandy lion. I was the only one that knew you could take the leg off on the near side, though it made no difference. I ducked in and whipped it off once before Molly had a bath, thinking that with her splashing around and all the water swishing the bath might tip over, and I'd be one up on her, but nothing happened.

So it was in the bathroom that I thought that if I had a decent bike of my own, nothing would matter much. I called out to Dad to wait for me, dashed up to the bedroom and grabbed my schoolbag, ran back to the kitchen, where Mum looked at me carefully. She was big and tall and solid, yet with a thinnish face that looked as though it didn't suit her, if you know what I mean. She really wasn't the thinnish type.

'You're a grubby little speck, Jimmy,' she said. 'Just look at your clothes. I'll have to give you clean ones for Father Gilligan tomorrow.'

I couldn't help grinnng at her, because no matter how she complained, I knew she was glad of the excuse to put me in clean clothes from top to bottom. I didn't mind putting up with being so darned clean because she got a great kick out of it, and I would see her looking at me as if she was enjoying herself.

She put her hands—they were big and strong hands— on my shoulders and pecked me on the cheek.

'Behave yourself,' she said. 'The sandwiches are cheese and egg.' She always said that, except that the cheese and egg wouldn't always be in the sandwiches.

I caught up with Dad at the gate, and together we set off down the road. He had his dark blue suit on this time,

29

and bowled along at a fast clip. I wanted to ask him about the bike, but couldn't for his talking. He seemed quite worked up and was giving me the old story; golly, I knew it by heart. His life story almost, and an interesting story, yet not when you hear it too often.

'Your mother hasn't been much help to me, Jimmy,' he said, 'but I'm not done yet. We Sullivans are not your ordinary common or garden Irish, no sir. Things haven't always been this way. Our branch of the family are high up; you should know that.'

It was a fine morning, the sun running sideways down to us, the air fresh and clean, so I skipped along, knocking at my schoolbag with my knee, not listening, hardly. I knew what he was saying without having to listen for anything except for when he stopped.

'Sullivan is an Irish name, but we're a British branch of the family. Family went to England from Ireland and made money there. Merchants. Not many Irish can do that. Then your great-grandfather came out to New Zealand and went farming. We were big people before the First World War, long before you were born.'

That was what got me; all this before I was born. It seems to me that if something happened before you were born you shouldn't let it worry you too much, unless it is history.

'Y'know, Dad, when I turn off I have nearly another mile to walk and you're almost at work,' I said.

'My father was well up, too, Jimmy, district chairman of the farmers' union and nearly a member of parliament,' he went on. 'I would have done all right, too, son, if it wasn't for the depression. It was bad luck, that was all. With this arm, I couldn't go farming. You realize your old man owned a couple of racehorses in the twenties. Travelled right around the country doing the race meetings. I was a wealthy man, and people, good people, I knew plenty of them. An Englishman, an aide to the governor-general, he was one of my best friends.

'Then there was the slump and that was that, and then I never did get a chance with that hotel in Wellington. Damned bad luck, that was all. I wasn't always a tally clerk; don't think that of your father.'

'It's a long way for me to walk,' I said.

'Your mother never helped me, Jimmy. I want you to know that,' he said. 'She was always pulling me down, never helping me, telling me I was no good. She wouldn't have anything to do with my friends, and they dropped me. That was the reason why. And I had nobody to give me a helping hand when things went wrong. She pulled me down, and you'll have to know that to understand some things.'

You would think I would have been interested when he spoke as he did at the end, because of how I felt, yet I wasn't. Whenever I heard any talk like that I became frightened and wanted to run away.

'Dad, I'm the only boy at school who hasn't got a bike,' I said, and jerked at his coat.

'What's all this?' he said, and I told him again.

'You ask your mother why you haven't one,' he said.

'Is a bike too expensive?' I asked. 'You aren't earning enough money?'

I was still half thinking of what Mum had said months before, and the words were hardly out of my mouth when he grabbed my shoulder and twisted me around. He stood looking down at me and looked as though he was going to blow up. The bald patch that ran back above the top of his head was red, even, and his eyes were squinted. Dad had never hit me, yet for a second there I thought he was going to give me a thick ear.

'Did your mother say that, eh?' he said, giving my shoulder a shake. 'Is that the kind of thing she says behind my back, that I can't earn enough money?'

My voice blocked up when I tried to answer. What I intended to say I don't know. Something was on the way out before it got stopped in my mouth.

Dad let go of my shoulder.

'You don't have to say anything, son; I know what kind of poison she spreads behind my back.'

Because it was the first and only time he had been really wild with me, I was frightened. Dad would lose his temper about all sorts of things, yet never with me. It wasn't as though there was much to upset him now, either; as a matter of fact, I didn't give a darn how much money he earned.

'You go on, Jimmy,' he said. 'Go on, go on. I've forgotten something I wanted to take to the office.'

'Come on, Pop,' I said as best I could. 'Don't go back now, please.'

'Off you go and don't argue,' he said, and turned and set off back, his right arm clipping to and fro, as though he was a soldier, if it wasn't for his other arm jiggling like that. He told me once his arm was hit in the war with the Germans. I was very young then, but I can remember what a laugh Mum got out of his saying that. 'It's a lot better than being kicked by a horse,' she said, 'even a racehorse.' After that, he wouldn't talk about his arm any more. People who get wounded in wars don't talk about it, that's why.

I felt rotten, watching him going back like that. It was like the time that Sniffy Peters and I started a small fire on Beach Street. We were going to bake some potatoes over the flames, when a whole row of toitoi bushes went up in smoke. Sniffy and I cleared off, of course, but hearing all the fuss, with the volunteer fire brigade ringing a bell as it came rushing out from Raggleton, made me feel queer inside.

By the time Dad had turned into the gate at home, I felt just as queer.

4

OUR house was on a metal road that ran along the line of the beach to the intersection, from where the streets were concreted. Our place was really off the proper streets, and for the first few hundred yards it took to get there you went past nothing but lupines and marram grass on either side. Some queer old rich old chap built the house long before for his health, and peace and quiet. He must have had it, too—as I mentioned before, the only sound was that of the sea.

I liked walking to the intersection down that metal road, being able to pluck at grass and lupines and stuff right there at the side of the road as you liked, and throw stones with all your might and not have to worry about hitting somebody on the head. Though there was that Saturday afternoon when Joe Waters and I were having a competition to see who could throw a stone the furtherest, and he tossed one away the dickens into the lupines and a woman yelped, and a red-haired man poked his head up and shook his fist, so we took off. I wanted to crawl back afterward and scout to see what the heck the two of them were doing in there, but Joe was worried in case he had really sconed the girl, and kept saying leave well enough alone, leave well enough alone, so we did.

It was a good area, that.

As I was saying, I watched Dad walking back until he had turned into the gate at home, and then I went on, feeling terrible, honestly. It was not often I felt terrible outdoors, I don't mind telling you; those fits, or whatever they were, that I had to keep off my protection tricks, they happened only inside at home.

But this morning, with Dad going off in a rage like that,

33

and with wondering what was going on, I felt as if I hadn't eaten for a week. I was a great one for my prayer and God, being pretty good at religion, and it was then I first thought of me and God, and I became irritable.

I had to tell him what I felt, so I waved my schoolbag over my head and shouted, 'You dirty bastard.' Boy, I bet that gave him a lot to think about. I felt better, too. When I finally got around to telling a priest about that in confession, not so long ago now, actually, he banged his head against the grille of the confessional, he was so surprised. Besides my not having confessed to it for over two years, he seemed to think that the sin was an unusually outstanding one, and for a while there I thought that he was personally going to toss me out of the church by the scruff of my neck. I got a little worried concerning the future of my education.

Anyway, as I was saying, I felt a whole lot better after shouting that out, and I dawdled along to school. It made me feel better in more ways than one, shouting to God, because I had discovered an outdoor protection trick. You've got to learn to protect yourself.

The indoor protection trick, the Hail Mary and washing and singing, I stumbled on when Mum and Dad had their first big row that I actually heard. Molly was in her first year at that boarding convent and I was eight and having the whole house to myself and I didn't like it as much as I expected. Molly was a darned nuisance being so bossy, yet I missed her. Mum and Dad had not been right for a long time, of course, but this was the first time I had heard them go on like that, and it was Dad's fault, blaming Mum for something she couldn't help. It was the time of that fat woman, too, and it certainly gives me a kick to think of her.

It happened the day we younger kids were given part of the day off at school because Sister Bernice was sick. There was nothing really wrong with her except an awful cold. She was sniffing and snuffling away like a penguin with hay fever.

I got home, and went bowling in the back door and there was this big fat woman in the kitchen. Fat, like five or six women rolled into one, and her legs bulged over her shoes as though she was going to spill out of them at any minute. She looked as though she was going to spill out of every darn thing she had on, as a matter of fact. There was a slight rip in the side of her dress, and I looked at it often, as I had the silly idea that should it start to split any more I had better get out of the room quickly, because only the week or so before I had been to the pictures and seen a dam bursting the same way.

'Hello,' I said. 'What's your name?'

She wheezed and huffed as she saw me, really surprised.

'And what's your name?' she squeaked. She had been washing her hands in the sink, and as she spoke she was drying them on a towel, and her great arms shook like billy-ho. I stared.

'Come on, where did you come from?' she squeaked again.

'I'm Jimmy, and I live here,' I said. 'Where's my mother?'

'Oh, oh,' she squeaked, and jiggled about. 'Oh, oh.'

She folded up the towel and put it in a small suitcase that was on the kitchen table. She took a small purse out of the case and from it lifted a sixpence between her fingers. Boy, with those fingers like sausages, it was the smallest looking sixpence I ever saw.

'I'm a friend of Mummy's,' she said. 'I dropped in to see her, and she's not feeling well, and she's having a nice long sleep. I'm just going, so why don't you walk down to Raggleton with me and I'll buy you an ice cream with this.'

Well, sixpence was a lot of money to me, and I thought it would be fun to walk along with a fat woman, so I went with her. I was going to go upstairs to see if Mum was really asleep, but she said not to, because I might wake her up. Then darn me if she didn't go waddling upstairs herself, shaking the whole house, and I sat in the kitchen eating a piece of cake I took from the cupboard, wondering what would happen if she fell through the ceiling. She hadn't handed over the sixpence yet, and I imagined her coming crashing down, and the money flying out of her hand, and then not being able to find it again.

She came back down the stairs puffing, and we set off to Raggleton.

'Have you ever been in a circus?' I asked.

'No,' she said in that high voice.

'You ought to think of it,' I said. 'You have the build, and think of all the wonderful people in a circus and travelling around from town to town. And the lions and the tigers and the elephants.'

'Have you ever had a whipping?' she said, squeaking so much that, honestly, she was like a queer kind of whistle blowing.

'No,' I said. 'I've had the strap a few times, though.'

'You only get whippings when you say nasty things to people,' she whistled. 'So be careful what you say.'

It wasn't very hot, yet she was starting to sweat as she walked, and the hand with which she held her suitcase looked as though it was swelling.

'Do you carry towels around in your case because you sweat easy?' I asked.

'I carry lots of things in this case, little brat,' she said. 'And when I meet nasty little boys I'm glad I do. I'm glad.'

'You don't have to worry about me being a nasty little boy,' I said. 'I'm pretty good. You are not too old for a circus are you?'

She didn't say a word, and the way she was puffing I guessed she was running out of wind.

'I suppose you would be hard on your clothes,' I said. 'Mum always says I'm hard on my clothes, and I suppose you would be, too. Even harder. All that weight pushing out all the time. And your shoes, too. I bet you are hard on your shoes, like I am.'

Still she didn't talk, so I breezed away, and asked her how she managed swimming—I was interested in whether

36

she could float, for instance. When we reached the intersection, she stopped, and really, she looked hot and
bothered. There were great patches of sweat down each side
of her dress, the rip in the side of which looked bigger than
ever, her big fat face was red, and she had black hairs on
her cheeks and under her nose, and I could see little wet
drops clinging to them.

'You're a very nasty little boy,' she squeaked. She took
another big breath and said, 'Go away, will you? Go away.
You go back to school and play, you little brute. You
naughty nasty little brute.'

'What about my sixpence?' I said, and you know, I felt
like crying because I knew she wasn't going to come across.

'Nothing for nasty little boys,' she said, and turned her
huge big back on me and heaved off.

I messed around there for a while, quite down in the
mouth, as I had been all set to have a good time with the
woman. Then I thought of the bad impression I had made
on her, and what she might tell my mother even though I
hadn't put a foot wrong, really, so I ran back home.

When I raced in the back door my mother called from
upstairs, 'Who's that?' You would think I was a burglar,
she sounded that frightened. 'It's me, Jimmy,' I called.
'Don't you come upstairs, don't you come upstairs,' she
shouted, as though I was worse than a burglar. 'You go
back to school. You go back to school or play. Don't you
come upstairs.' Then a door banged, and the house was
so quiet I could hear my breathing.

I went back to school, because I had left my bag there,
anyway, with my lunch in it, and then I wandered around,
not being able to find even Joe Waters. I ended up at the
beach and I don't mind saying I was lonely, until I thought
of Bloody Jack. I went and sat down at the wharf and
shared my sandwiches with him. I told him about the fat
woman, and he got indignant and said that the police would
lock her up one day if they ever caught her, and he patted
me on the neck with his hand. I assured him that I didn't

mind being called a nasty little boy, and that she wasn't that bad.

When I got home, Mum called out to me to come upstairs, and I found the bedroom door open and she in bed, white as a sheet. She said she was sorry she had stopped me coming to see her in the morning, but she hadn't wanted to worry me. I made her a cup of tea, which she said was very good, and that pleased me immensely.

Dad came home and hit the roof. He called the doctor, who turned up in a big car, stayed for about ten minutes, and then left. I was hanging around the foot of the stairs as he came down and he looked very bad-tempered.

As soon as he was gone, I heard Dad shouting. At the top of his voice, shouting, on and on, and I sat on the bottom stair feeling—well, I don't know how I felt. I won't say what he said; at least I don't remember, they were such queer names. He was blaming her for being sick, and she kept repeating, 'I'm forty, do you hear? I'm forty and I've been through enough. I'm forty, it was too much.' Their voices were over the whole house, as though they were in each room shouting at each other. I stood up and walked up the passage, and the whole house became silent, all the voices fading, and I stopped and tried to listen, yet there was no sound left. The air started to get cold and feel thick about me. I turned to the passage wall and lifted up my arms and rested them against the wallpaper, and looked at all those whirling designs there, and tried to think about them. It was no use; I was feeling worse, as if there was some crust about me. I thought of Sister Bernice telling us what a great help the Hail Mary was, and at the same time I thought that if I washed myself, I would be all right. So I got along to the bathroom, and as I went I did begin to hear something, my heart, bumping. I said the Hail Mary out loud and washed myself down, and I began to feel much better, and then I sang a song, 'It's a Long Way to Tipperary'. That came to me out of the blue.

Dad came downstairs and went out of the house slamming

doors. I went to my bedroom and stayed there till I was hungry. Then I went out to the kitchen and ate some bread and butter and went to bed. I heard Mum call out while I was in the kitchen, and I didn't answer.

Since that time I always used those protection tricks when I had those fits, and they worked.

Mum was out of bed in a few days, and I didn't let on I heard what she and Dad had said to each other. I started to talk about the fat woman, though, and she made me promise never to say a word about her to anyone, which was tough on me. I mean she was the fattest woman in the world, I suppose, and I wasn't allowed to talk about her, even at school.

You can see that when I started feeling terrible out-of-doors, it was a great help for me to discover that by shouting at God I could make myself feel a lot better.

5

AFTER Dad had gone back home that morning, leaving me to go on by myself, I went on to school, of course, and it was one of my funny days there. I can't complain, I suppose, because I was very clever, and generally top of my class, so I could afford to go funny, not that I ever did deliberately. I wouldn't even know it had happened till school started, and I would try to pay attention, only to find my brain going off in all directions at once. Honestly, those times it was hard for me to think of what two and two might be.

That day I looked around the class with a feeling they were all strangers. Or, at least, that I was a stranger to them. Even Joe Waters, in many ways my best friend, looked strange at the next desk, with his hair sticking up like a hedgehog, and his ears sticking out, and that grin on his face that was there even when he was serious, his teeth were so prominent. Even Joe, with all those features, looked so strange that when I realized that I knew his name it was an enomous relief to me, as it would be a terrible fix to forget names of people you know.

There was Joseph Kane, the fat boy, Hector Simpson, whose father used to play representative football, Sniffy Peters, and Legs Hope, all my friends, and yet I hardly knew them. We sat there in our room, separated by a folding door from the younger kids—our school was really one big hall, partitioned off by these doors. We were in the top classes, standard five and six, you know, and I, even though I was eleven and in standard five, was just as smart as some of the chaps in standard six. So I came in for some attention. You can see these funny periods could be awkward for me, and I used to have to pretend not to be feeling well. Once I told Sister the truth, that my brain wasn't functioning

40

properly, when she asked me a question, and she thought I was making a fool of her. So after that when I got stuck I always said I was ill, and moped over my desk, sniffing and rubbing my head as though I was sick as a dog.

Even the room was strange with its holy pictures on the walls, the two blackboards on their easels up front, the big fireplace on the side, and the mantelpiece which Sister Angela always had decked with flowers to commemorate some saint, as often as not Saint Francis. I had to look around, study the views out the window on each side wall, as well as everything inside, to try and get myself in sight. Outside the right window was the playground, and you could see part of the town in the distance; on the other side was a small hill neatly covered by pine trees, a good place for games.

But if I steered my thinking, all I could see were Dad and Mum back home fighting over that bike I wanted. So I gave up, and just let my mind wander. In my mind I went for a flight in an aeroplane, and looked down on Raggleton from high up. I had a pilot, of course, a man in a leather jacket and goggles, and he swooped the plane down low over the beach, and everybody I knew was down there waving up at us. I had just got to the part where the pilot was turning to me and saying, 'You've got flying in your blood, I can see that; would you like to take over the controls?' when I felt a hard prod on my shoulders and, looking up, I saw Sister Angela standing over me.

'Will you give me the answer, please, Jimmy?'

I said, 'I didn't hear the question properly, Sister.'

'I know you didn't, dreamer. I'm teaching history. Leave your dreaming till after school.'

The rest of the class tittered away and I felt a darn fool. I did my best to follow lessons the rest of the morning, and in case I was caught again, I started to try and look as though I was sick.

In the lunch hour we played seven-a-side football and I kicked a field goal. It was a better kick than Joe Waters, who was really the best kick in the whole school, had made for weeks, and during the afternoon I thought of myself as a great footballer, really setting games on fire and tearing the opposition into shredded wheat. Even though I was only a kid I was picked to represent the country in an international match, and my photograph was in the papers, and all the kids at school got seats in the grandstand to watch me play, and my mother and father were so pleased they came to watch me.

I was so wrapped up in this dream that when I did hear Sister Angela I thought she was calling me from the grandstand.

'Jimmy, will you stand up and tell the class what I have been talking about?'

I stood up and looked at her.

'You haven't been listening, have you?'

'No, Sister.'

She sighed and looked down at the desk and closed her eyes. She was saying a short prayer. She always did before she strapped anybody.

'Come out here, Jimmy.'

I went out, feeling somehow pleased with what was going to happen. I was being looked at by everybody, even Jesus with his bleeding heart seemed to be looking, and the windows on the side walls, they were not looking out, they were looking in, and at me; honestly, I got as much kick out of it as Jesus did at the crucifixion.

Sister had taken the single black strap, split in two at the end, from the drawer of her desk, and was looking at me. Anybody could see that she was soft and didn't like what she was going to do.

'You must pay attention, Jimmy,' she said.

'Yes, Sister.'

'Hold out your hand.'

By holding your hand high, you could cut off a lot of the force out of the strap, but I held my hand low. She swung the strap over her shoulder and slapped it down

42

hard. My hand stung, and felt as though it was scorched. She hit me once more, and then dropped her arm, the strap dangling in her grip. I kept my hand out, and said to her in my mind, 'Go on, hit me again, go on.' She could have gone on hitting me till kingdom come and I would still be holding out my hand when she stopped, that's the way I felt.

'That's all, Jimmy,' she said. She was puffing slightly, and anybody could see she was soft.

'Thank you, Sister,' I said loudly, and walked back to my desk holding my hand at my side as though it didn't hurt, and winking to the class. Once the class started again I nursed the hand in my lap, and blew on it a few times when nobody was looking.

6

I DIDN'T want to go home straight away after school. I went
with Joe Waters and Sniffy Peters up to the top of that
small hill next to the school. It was a fine afternoon, the hot
of the day wearing down till all was nicely warm and drowsy.
We decided we would sit on top of the hill and talk. Sniffy
was almost as good a friend of mine as Joe was, even though
he was too good-looking. He had curly black hair and skin
like a girl's, long eyelashes and the rest, and he was always
clean, no matter what. Even after a mud fight, he was tidy
and neat and, darn me, he never got any muck under his
nails, either. Yet he wasn't sissy, and didn't run away from
fights. We called him Sniffy because his mother made him
carry two handkerchiefs, and not because he sniffed any
more than the rest of us. I wouldn't be surprised if he sniffed
less.

'What was wrong with you today, Jimmy?' Sniffy asked
as we climbed up the hill. 'Sister was looking at you all day
and I knew you would get it if you didn't watch out.'

'You showed her,' Joe said. 'You didn't even blink. Only
trouble is that from now on, instead of giving us two bangs
with the old strap, she'll give us three, because she'll think
two is not enough.'

'For all I care,' I said, 'she can give me fifty bangs.'

'Gee,' said Joe, 'fifty bangs would make you sit up and
take notice.'

'I could take fifty bangs without blinking,' said Sniffy.
'Think of what you would have to do to get fifty bangs,
though. That would be the really hard part. You'd have to
murder somebody.'

We reached the top of the hill quickly as soon as we
were clear of the pine trees on the slope, and lay down on

the ground. We could see the whole of Raggleton on one side, all the houses and even the shopping centre, looking lazy as if it was sun-bathing beside the sea. Behind the town we could see the wharf, with a few boats tied up alongside, and one man up a mast, painting. I wasn't sure, but at one end, in a shadow, I thought I could make out Bloody Jack, fishing as usual.

Joe grinned, and boy, with all his teeth, when he grinned you really knew he was grinning.

'Dopey Sniffy,' he said. 'If you murdered somebody, they wouldn't give you the strap. They'd hang you or put you in jail for always and always at least.'

'Well, what would they give you fifty bangs for?' asked Sniffy. 'What's the use of Jimmy saying Sister could give him fifty bangs if there isn't nothing she could give him fifty bangs for?'

'He could break all the windows at school and saw her desk in half, that might do it,' said Joe. 'Even then, I daresay, he'd get the bangs on the instalment plan, as they call it. My mother says that if something is too much at once they give it to you on the instalment plan.'

'I just mentioned murder as a metaphor or simile or one of those figures of speech,' Sniffy said. 'Nobody would be fool enough to think I really meant it really, if you know what I mean. It was just an expression.'

There we were, the three of us, in our navy-blue shorts and shirts, Joe with his teeth and ears and hair sticking out, and Sniffy looking like an angel, and me, all sitting there and not knowing a darn thing. Me, what did I look like, I wonder? My ears stuck out like Joe's, I admit, but my hair was tidier. I was not as thick as the other two were. Not skinny, no sir; lean was a good word for my condition. I was the smartest, too. That's why I got tired of the conversation first, as I could see what goats we were in our short pants and all, talking such stuff.

'Shut up, both of you,' I said. 'You don't know what you're talking about,'

'Well, what should we talk about?' asked Joe. 'You mention something else, because you started us off before with your skite about not caring about fifty bangs and now you say shut up. You start a new subject then.'

'Wrestling,' said Sniffy. 'Let's talk wrestling holds.'

They were both looking at me, waiting for me to give the word.

'Let's talk about our mothers and fathers,' I said.

You should have seen them. They didn't react at all. You would think they were still waiting for me to speak.

'What?' said Sniffy.

'Mothers and fathers. Parents,' I said.

'What do you mean, mothers and fathers?' said Joe.

'What I said. Let's talk about them.'

'What is there to talk about?' said Sniffy.

Honestly, the pair of them were looking at me as though I was loopy. I nearly couldn't even see Joe's teeth, that's how serious he looked.

'Don't you ever think about your parents?' I asked, trying hard to get them interested. 'What they are like, and how they go on.'

'You usually have pretty good ideas, Jimmy,' said Joe. 'But this beats the band. Parents? There's your mother and father and they're . . . well, they're there. What is there to talk about?'

Sniffy's face brightened, and he said, 'You mean about what our fathers can do? Like Heck Simpson's father being a footballer once. You mean about fathers, don't you? Mothers are mothers, they are, but fathers do something else besides.'

'No,' I said. 'Mothers and fathers together, I mean.'

The pair of them lost interest there, and didn't ask me anything more. They were good friends and didn't like to hurt my feelings, I suppose, especially as I had got the strap that day.

'Forget about it then. I don't care. It struck me as an interesting subject, that's all. I thought you might have something interesting to say, that's all.'

'What about war?' said Joe. 'Let's talk about war, and what it would be like to be shot or blown up or gassed or hit on the head with the wrong end of a gun.'

'O.K.,' said Sniffy.

'O.K.,' I said.

We kids must have sat up on that hill for an hour talking away, and in that time the weather changed. Big black clouds came bowling in from over the sea, the wind grew cold, and we could see the whole town starting to shiver. We came down as soon as it began to spit with rain, and ran back to the intersection where we split up and went our different ways home. It was well after four o'clock when I got home. Of course I was worrying whether Mum would blame me for making Dad get into such an awful temper in the morning. Going inside was a bit like going to school the day of exams. But Mum didn't notice me; she was moving around the house with a duster, wrapped up in thought, as they say in books. So without saying anything I put my boots on, took my raincoat from the bedroom door, and went off to see Bloody Jack.

As I got near the wharf I could see him sitting there staring into the water, the collar of his old coat right up and his head pulled down so far into it that I could only see bits of dirty white hair sticking out the top, and the end of his nose sticking out front. The only other part of him that was showing was his thumb and finger sticking out of his sleeve holding his fishing line. And the wind was bashing the water into the piles of the wharf, with spray kicking up everywhere, and outside the harbour the sea was sucking and heaving away as though a million mad whales were underneath. I had to admire Bloody Jack for sitting on there even though he didn't have a dog's show of getting any fish.

When I got to him, though he was huddled up like that, I could see he didn't have any more clothes on than usual, as he always wore the dirty old coat. When I asked him why, it didn't seem to worry him that this was the first thing

47

I said to him. He told me he was wearing two sets of underwear.

'Close to your skin is the place to lick the cold,' he said. 'No use at all messing around trying to keep the elements out when your clothes are already on. You make a burden of yourself to carry around, that's all.'

I sat down beside him. My heavy boots dragged on my feet as I dangled them over the edge of the wharf. Jack's fishing line was swinging up and down in the swells. Little bits of spray were sneezing up from the water into my face. It was a heck of a time to be there, really.

'You're a funny mite,' said Bloody Jack. 'I'm a funny old chap but I got the right to be, but you're a funny young chap and that's different.'

'What do you mean?' I said, a bit flustered. 'There's nothing funny about me, nothing funny at all. There's nothing funny about you, or either of us.'

'Don't get on your high horse, boy,' he said. 'I was thinking of how you're always wandering around like a lost lamb, and like to sit and talk with me so much. I like you to sit and talk with me, and then I think, is it good for you like?'

'Other boys talk with you.'

'Sure they do—for a while. Then they drift off when they've had a good look at me, and don't worry me any more.'

'Would you rather I didn't bother you then?'

The lower part of his face, covered with all that black fuzz, moved as though it was going to twist up around his big hooked nose, and as his funny dim old eyes peered down at me big drips of spray ran over his forehead.

'Don't you talk no damn nonsense,' he said. 'No damn nonsense now. I like you hanging around, but what does your Dad and Mum think, eh?'

'They don't care what I do. They don't worry.'

There must have been something in the way I said that because he pushed his face down a little closer, as if to get

48

a good look at me, and said, 'What's that now? You don't get along with your Mum and Dad?'

'They don't get along with each other,' I said. 'They don't get along much at all.'

There was a such a gust of wind then, stinging wet, and I shivered closer to Jack, and got a whiff of his khaki sweater, a mixture of fish and tobacco smells, and the wind was like a whip banging near my cold ears, and the wharf shook slightly beneath us. I got a loopy feeling that the sea and the wind and the sky were God shaking his finger at me for telling on my mother and father, and I yelled out, 'I don't care.'

The wind dropped, and Jack said, 'You've got troubles the way I didn't expect, young'un,' he said. 'You mean your Mum and Dad fight? Throw things at each other and the like of that?'

'No, they just talk back and forth, and sometimes they shout and I feel terrible.'

'Like what for instance?'

'I don't know,' I said. 'Dad drinks, you know, and Mum gets iffy. It's been going on ever since I can remember, I suppose, but these last two years it's worse. Dad keeps saying she dragged him down, and she says back that he never was up. Dad's halfway always talking about how he hasn't got on in the world the way he should of, and it wasn't his fault, it was hers, and the depression's. They go on like that and I can't understand, really I can't, what it's all about, and yet I feel terrible.'

I took a deep breath then, and realized that still the wind was keeping down, and the splattering of the sea had stopped, and that even a seagull was hanging over the water, wing way out and not moving, and the wharf was steady as a rock, as if everything was keeping quiet to hear me talk. I didn't care, though. I went on.

'And Mum has changed a lot, and she's not the same. She goes around the house sometimes as though nobody else lives there but her, not even me, and she has a funny

49

look in her eyes. She is friendly to me and her eyes are all right then. She's been that way ever since she was sick that time. She looks as though she picked up sixpence and lost a pound note as they say. That was silly, her getting sick, and he blaming her for getting sick.'

'It's hard to say when people are being silly,' said Jack. 'Little boys don't understand what is going on, and perhaps they should not pay attention. Grownups should be ignored sometimes, kind of, by children.'

'It's hard not to pay attention,' I explained, 'especially when they shout. Do you think I'm queer and imagine things?' I said.

'No, it's not that,' said Jack. 'You're hearing right, I don't doubt a second. It's just that you're hearing what you shouldn't be. Most of the trouble in the world starts that way, Jimmy, with people hearing or seeing something they shouldn't be. You think if you never bothered to look or see anything much you wouldn't be worrying.'

'I'd have to be very dumb to be like that,' I said.

'Then be dumb,' he said. 'See nothing, hear nothing.'

'I can't, I can't,' I said. 'I can't help hearing. I can't help seeing. I can't help it unless I run away.'

'Then just don't care,' said Jack. 'Don't care. Like for instance you know about that fire down at Albertville a couple of days ago and six people got burned to death?'

I nodded my head. Everybody knew about that fire. We'd even talked about it at school.

'Well,' said Jack. 'You know about the fire, and yet it doesn't drive you out of your head thinking about it, does it?'

'No,' I said. 'I'm sorry, even so.'

'Of course you are sorry, but you don't care. Well, be the same with your Mum and Dad. Be sorry but don't worry or care. They can take care of themselves. They both are nice to you aren't they?'

'Yes.'

'That's all you got to worry about then. They're nice to you. Let them worry about the other business.'

50

'I'll try,' I said.

We were both quiet after that, with old Jack just staring down into the water around his line as though he could see the fish, and me looking everywhere at once. Then I thought that I would ask him about his troubles, if he had any, seeing he was so decent about mine. With that advice and stuff.

'Don't you worry about a thing, Jack?' I asked.

'Nope,' he said.

'What about being all by yourself, and nobody to look after you, as you told me once you had no family?'

He moved his chin up and around and jerked at his line.

'Nope,' he said. 'Don't worry.'

'You mean you never worried?' I said, wondering if he thought I had been a little sissy for telling him what I had earlier.

'Worried a long time ago about my wife. All of thirty years ago it must be. Worried myself nearly sick. Then she ran away and I never did see her again and I never did worry much again, either. He was a fat little bloke with a beard, all the time dressing up, and having smelly oil on his hair, thinking he was a great one, he was.'

'Who was?' I asked.

'He was,' he said.

That was Bloody Jack all over. He was always getting mixed up like that, without making sense, when he talked about himself. So I tried another subject.

'What about when you can't fish any more, as people can't when they get too old,' I explained to him.

'I'm old now, son,' he said. 'And it doesn't worry me. And it never will. I've got me pension and I've got me fishing and I've got the sea. They'll never have to bury me, either. I know these tides too well for that.'

'You're a great one not to worry,' I said, just to end the conversation. I liked Jack, and liked talking to him, yet he never meant much. I suppose his advice about my mother and father was good, but when he talked so queer at the same time I lost confidence in it. You mightn't understand that, how I liked hearing him talk, without going much for what he actually said. I remember thinking that if he talked nonsense about himself, what he said about me and my parents was probably nonsense, too.

Yet Bloody Jack was the only one I ever talked to about my parents. I never could talk to my sister Molly, because she was loopy.

7

I SUPPOSE by the way I talk you would think I was the only child in our family. But I don't really forget my sister Molly. She is six years older than me, and I must admit she seems to have done what she said she would do. She still writes to me pretty regularly, too, so I know she can't forget me, either. I read in a magazine the other day of two people who were the only ones to come out alive when a ship sank about forty years ago, and ever since they have written to each other, even though they were strangers at the time. Perhaps Molly and I are going to be like that.

Having a sister six years older than you are isn't what it is cracked up to be, really. Molly always disappointed me because she didn't make much sense, wasn't much help. She never knew about Mum and Dad. If she had only known, things might have been different between us, but I could never talk to her about it.

I remember years ago, when she was fourteen or so, back after her first year at boarding-school, that Sacred Heart Convent at Wellington, and had been home for a week or more. I knew that she was growing up, because I had gone up to her room to wake her up in the morning, and she was sound asleep on her back, even snoring a little, and I jerked the blankets right back off her, and there she was with her nightdress up around her neck. It was a shock to me, that, her starting to be like a woman, so I turned around and took off out of the room like a rocket. I don't know when she got to waking up; when she became cold, I suppose.

She had fair hair, turned-up nose, blue eyes, and everybody said she was very pretty, even though she was thin and didn't fill out till later. Her eyes were so big, and they looked at you so nicely that it seemed that she would never touch you, except with a wand.

'Do you like mother or father the best?' she said as we went to the beach that afternoon. She had promised to go swimming with me, and it wasn't far from home to the sea by the short cut. We were in our swimming togs, having changed before leaving.

'What do you mean?' I asked.

'Do you like mother and father?'

I don't know what she had at the back of her mind, probably some stupid grievance, and I became afraid that she would find out what had been going on at home while she had been at school.

She didn't know anything, Molly didn't. And I knew I wasn't supposed to, either, and it was the last thing she would find out from me.

'They're both all right,' I said.

'They're not, Jimmy, and you shouldn't say so. I hate them, and you should hate them.'

'All right,' I said. 'I hate them.'

'Why do you hate them?' she asked. 'It's no use hating them if you don't know why. You have to know why; you can't just say it. It's better to know early so you can get used to the idea.'

It took me a while to get around that one. It was late afternoon, and the sun was still hot; there was nobody but us on the beach, and the sea was rolling up and swishing to within a few inches of our feet. It was a silly time to be talking the way she was.

'I hate them because you've got new swimming togs and I haven't,' I said.

'Oh, you're a stupid little boy,' she said, and smacked a bare foot into the sand. 'I don't know why I waste my time on you.'

Her voice got very high, and she put a hand on top of my head and pushed it from side to side. She wasn't mad in her usual way, either. She was plain silly. And then she began to cry. The tears rolled down her face, and she gulped as though she was about to choke.

'I'm sorry,' I said. 'I don't mind you having new togs. After all, you did grow out of your last ones, and mine still fit me.'

She sat down and bent her face down and rubbed it hard with her hands. She rubbed her eyes with her fingers, and then both her cheeks, as though she was scrubbing off dirt. She was so white and spidery-looking sitting down there, all arms and legs.

'Let's go for a swim,' I said. 'You'll feel a lot better in the water.'

I am willing to admit now that I felt glad she was crying. Yet once I felt glad I wanted her to stop. But at first, even though she looked like a white golliwog with half the stuffing taken out of it, flopped on the sand and no sign of anybody to pick it up, I didn't mind.

I walked around her, and when she was quiet I took a handful of warm sand and poured it over her shoulders.

'Take me in for a swim. That's what you brought me down here for,' I said.

She got up as if nothing had happened and took me by the hand and together we walked into the water. The water was really warm, yet it was cold when it first hit your skin, and I jumped up and down. Molly tightened her grip on my hand and kept on walking out as though she wasn't even feeling the water. In a matter of seconds it was up to my waist and I threw myself forward and went under, head and all.

'You float and I'll push you out past the breakers,' said Molly, sliding into the water beside me.

The sea was very calm, and the swells were hardly breaking, just frothing slightly as they curled. It was easy going, as I floated on my back kicking my feet, and Molly pushed me along, up and over the rollers, till the water was up to her neck, and then swinging her up out of her depth. She was a good swimmer and I wasn't frightened; water never frightened me. I lay there, seeing the dark blue sky and feeling the sun, like a ship at sea, a small ship at sea, and Molly was steering me. My feet splashed and her arms dipped and pushed as she swam sidearm alongside me. I turned my head slightly and I could see her face beside my shoulders, and she and I were the friendliest we had ever been.

Her hair was wet and clinging to her head, and her big eyes were looking at me in a very nice way. It couldn't have been very long we were like that, yet I've always remembered those moments. And really, when I think of Molly, that is one of the times that come back to me.

'Do you love me, Jimmy?' she asked in a funny voice.

I laughed and got some water in my mouth and was about to give her some cheek when I thought of how mean I had been about not being sorry she had cried.

'Yes,' I said. 'Of course.'

She closed her eyes, and opened them again, and it was as though she had changed inside as she blinked, there was so much difference in her look.

'Let's go on and on and not go back,' she said. 'That'll show them.'

'You can't swim for ever, you're not that good,' I said.

'It doesn't make any difference.'

'Silly thing,' I said.

I stopped kicking and just waggled my hands around. She dug her fingers into my chest with the hand she was steering me with, and let herself sink until her hair was floating underneath my shoulder like seaweed. She came up again and wriggled her mouth up to my ear, as though she was whispering to me in the dark, and said, 'Please come with me, Jimmy. I'd be frightened by myself.'

I splashed back from her with a couple of kicks and turned over on my stomach. She was looking so red and puffy and silly-looking that I thought it best not to talk any more; besides, I wasn't good enough to talk and swim at the same time. I took a deep breath and started paddling back to the beach.

56

We were too far out for me to get back by myself, but she let me battle away alone till I was nearly tired out before she came and helped.

'Float again, stupid,' she said. I turned on my back and she slipped her arm underneath me and pushed me forward. It was some strain for her, too, because she was puffing loudly and blowing by the time we got back to where the water was shallow enough for her to stand and walk as she held me up.

When I could stand, I said, 'You still think you can swim forever?' and she pushed me right under.

'That's for being a big coward,' she said when I came up.

We went back to the beach and walked along to where we had left our towels. I sat down, and Molly sat beside me and dried my face and head, and then I dried her back. As I did, I think she cried again. I say I think, because I couldn't really see, and I kept on rubbing, not wanting to get mixed up with her sloppiness. Then she lay down with her face in her arms in the sand and I did the same.

It doesn't seem much, that, yet that was the time I was friendliest with Molly, even though she was so silly. She wasn't at home when the trouble was on, and she certainly wasn't there at the end, and I really don't think she cared, not knowing as much as I did. Her saying how she hated mother and father was silly, because they hadn't done anything to her. It was probably because she couldn't have a new dress or something just about as stupid. She was a little loopy and sloppy about herself like that. That bit about her wanting to swim on forever was just like her. She used to race me sometimes and give me a start and still beat me, and then say she could beat anyone. There was nothing she wouldn't say she could do. And she was always telling me how much I had to learn, and how much she knew. Golly, once there she went to a fancy-dress ball as a queen, and and I had to be her page. Wouldn't that beat the band?

Yet I liked her that time on the beach. I suppose it was

because she treated me as an equal. And it was great to float on your back in a calm sea and have somebody steer you.

8

'WHAT did you think of that fire at Albertville?' I asked Mum after tea.

'Mmm?' she said.

'The fire at Albertville,' I said.

'It was terrible,' she said. 'All those people.'

'Yes, all those people getting burned up like that. You feel sorry, but you don't get knocked out by it, though, do you? I mean it's all right not to feel knocked out by it, isn't it? I would feel worse actually if I bashed my hand with a hammer or something. Is that all right?'

I was going to ask her a few more questions, but the flat old way she spoke showed me she wasn't interested, so I stopped. I was home after that time with Bloody Jack on the wharf and for the first time I was starting to feel like my old self. She hadn't said much to me at all, which was a relief in some ways.

As I came back from the wharf I had remembered how silent Mum had been when I was first home from school, and it came to me that perhaps she blamed me for Dad going back in a rage that morning. There was that blasted wind blowing away, and me leaning into it, pushing slowly up the road, slowly, with the lupines and marram grass shaking and rustling at the edge of the footpath, and baby handfuls of sand spattering into me, and it getting dark and a long time since I had eaten anything. Yet I didn't much want to go home.

But no matter how slowly you go, you always get home, and no matter how much you can duck, you can't duck what is going to happen. Only this night nothing happened. Not at first. Dad wasn't home, Mum was still silent, and I never said anything much, and neither did she.

She had a routine, of course, in that big house, running it and all that, and no doubt there was plenty to think about and mothers can't talk to their children all the time, and I didn't mind, really. Once I was inside, in fact, and had been in the kitchen for a while, and her still silent, not saying anything, it was a relief, because I knew she wasn't going to mention the bike business. That was a weight off my mind.

She moved about the kitchen, and I always got quite a kick watching her there. She would do this, and do that, from the stove to the sink, lifting lids off pots, opening cupboard doors, rattling plates, opening the stove door and letting big puffs of steam out from whatever was cooking. And making the table, up and across with the cloth, on with the knives and forks and spoons, and all the rest, so quick, it was done in the blink of an eye. You only had to watch her about the kitchen to know she was good at it. I seem to remember one of her women friends telling her she had the cleanest cupboards in the whole of Raggleton.

Even Dad told me once that she was a wonderful housekeeper. It got so that I used to just watch her, knowing she was something of a champion at it. I actually told her she was a champion. I suppose a kid likes to think his mother and father are champions in some respect. There was a kid at school once who skited that his mother had really big legs, though I don't see that it was much to skite about. It shows you, though.

So I didn't mind her not talking, and I watched her getting my tea, and all we said was pass this and pass that please, thank you, and excuse me, with her adding a few more words like more of this or more of that, and me saying thanks.

She was big, as I have probably said, and strong-looking, and her hair was straight and shining and she had a face some people would say was too long—in fact, when I was a tiny kid I seem to remember her saying that people said just that—and big brown eyes. But now I am getting her mixed up.

60

I suppose it's because I can think of three of her. As she was long, long ago; she was full of beans then, tossing me into the air so high, and laughing so loud, with big bright eyes, shiny black hair, and a face that had a lot of bone in it. Some faces are soft and fleshy and you would never guess there was any bone there, but in her face you could see the bone under the smooth skin, around her cheeks, and on her forehead, and around her jaw, which I daresay was somewhat longer than most. Once, there, I saw a picture of the Duke of Wellington, and he reminded me a little of my mother in the face. Whether it was before or after the Battle of Waterloo in 1815 I can't say. Long ago her skin was smooth, and she was bright-eyed, and when her arms lifted me I felt very weak and comfortable indeed.

The second picture I have of her is at the time I'm talking about. I said her hair was straight and shining, and that was wrong—it used to shine, I meant. Now it was just straight hair, and I would think what a pity she didn't wash and comb it more often to make it the way it used to be. And the skin puckered up a little somehow, and her face seemed thinner, and her eyes were still nice eyes, yet they made me a little scared sometimes, looking very hot and bothered, or staring away and not blinking and not looking.

The third picture is my business. I'm not sure that I remember it, anyway, because more and more I see her as she was at first. Why isn't everybody and everything the way they were at first? I wonder.

After tea was finished, I dried the dishes for her. That was when I asked about the Albertville fire. Up till then, as I said before, I had been a bit worried that she would blame me for Dad tearing back home this morning, like a bat out of hell, as they say; it would have been awful if she had blamed me for starting another big row. Not that my wanting a bike was wrong, really; it just seemed to have the wrong results, that's all. Nobody could really blame me.

Our sink took up most of one side of the kitchen, with great big cupboards underneath, and plenty of room on top to stack stuff. And the sink itself was so deep Mum would have to put her arms in water up past her elbows to reach the bottom when it was full.

I stood beside her with a big white tea towel and though usually I could never dry dishes as fast as she could wash them, I didn't have any trouble keeping up with her this night.

And then she said, out of the blue, 'How would you like to go away for a holiday, Jimmy?'

I nearly dropped a cup.

'Golly, what for?' I said.

She didn't even look back at me as I looked up at her. She looked on into the steam rising from the water, her hair a little damp and hanging down each side of her face as she was leaning over the dishes, as if she hadn't said a word.

'That's a funny thing to say,' I said. 'This is only the middle of the year and everybody knows you don't take holidays till the end of the year when school finishes.'

She looked at me now, and gave a funny smile.

'I had a letter from Molly and she has made some friends in Wellington who have a little brother the same age as you, and Molly says they would like you to go and stay with them for a few days.'

'When did the letter from Molly come?' I asked. 'This is Tuesday and she writes on Sunday, posts on Monday, and we get them on Wednesday.'

'It came this afternoon, son—she must have posted it early.'

'Where is it?' I asked. I always liked to read Molly's letters, and now and then I would write one to her myself. Not very long ones, and mainly to give her some cheek.

'This is one she wrote only to Mummy about a private matter. It is not for your eyes.'

That really rocked me. Molly had never done anything like that before.

'Well, she has no darned right to go suggesting things

62

like that behind my back,' I said. 'If silly old Molly wants to go writing letters behind my back, and not letting me see them, then she had better not write about me, that's all.'

Mum gave a sigh, and murmured, 'Now, now, boy. Forget I ever mentioned it. Molly thought it might be nice for you.'

I told her that what Molly thought was nice for me was most unlikely to be what I thought would be nice for me, and I went on like that for quite some time. I really felt mad as a wet hen, although I didn't quite know why. I felt it was a queer time for Mum to raise the matter, too, rather like tossing a cupful of cold water on somebody when they are sitting in a hot bath.

She did not say anything more, other than that the subject was closed, and I finished the drying, watching her out of the corner of my eye, the way I did at school when one of the kids threatened to poke a ruler into my ribs. And then I began to feel frightened, looking at her like that, and she not smiling: she had a kind of black dress on, but over the top she was wearing a great big sack apron—she always wore that when she washed up—and in that steam, with the light not strong, and her leaning on her big arms into the water, she reminded me of a picture in a history book of the executioner who killed one of the kings: he had a leather apron on, and was looking down at the chopping block.

9

MY schoolbooks were before me, and I actually did get some homework done after that. I sat in the lounge, at one end of the polished table, with my back to the wall, able to see the whole room. I always did my school home-work there, so that when I looked away from my books I had something to look at, if you know what I mean. I think I worked better there, too: I could see the brown carpet on the floor, with a dull red leafy pattern, and the furniture so arranged that you would have to get down on your hands and knees to see the worn patches, or lift up the deerskin in front of the fireplace. The walls were still pretty clean. They were what made me first realize that Dad had some-thing really wrong with his arm. When I was about five or thereabouts Mum wanted new wallpaper. Dad said he would be damned if she was going to make him a one-armed paperhanger. So he whitewashed the walls, instead.

And the furniture was good, too. Polished wood chairs with the table at which I sat, a big brown sofa with a couple of easy chairs to match, and an odd big old black armchair that was in the house even before we moved in, I believe. On the mantelpiece above the fireplace at the other end of the room was a hefty clock that whirred away and shook without actually striking on the hour, the chimes being broken, a picture of Molly and I when I was a baby, a small brass statue of a fat Chinaman sitting on his rump in a loose dressing gown that was undone enough to show his belly button and a chest that looked more like a woman's in some respects; he was squatting on a hollow base that held pins and other small junk. Also on the mantelpiece were a heavy bowl that was always full of geraniums, an ivory elephant about the size of a kitten, a jug that was made like the face of a very happy man indeed, and which could be made to play 'Auld Lang Syne' if you wound up the works at the bottom, a pack of cards that nobody used now that Molly was away, and a few odds and ends. Above the mantelpiece was a tremendous picture of a huge stag on the top of a small hill sniffing the air in a very proud fashion, with miles of misty countryside and a lake down below him.

What interested me this night was the writing bureau in the corner to the right of the fireplace. I knew that Molly's letter would be there, for Mum put letters there when she finished reading them, even the bills. I looked up at the bureau, and, honestly, all the fancy carvings on it, even the curly woodwork that mounted the top, started to look like the shape of Molly's handwriting. It was a big hunk of furniture, that bureau, with a writing place hanging down from it like a tray on the end of two pieces of light chain, and all the slots stuffed with papers, letters, and the rest— Mum kept her cotton there, too. And right at the top left-hand hole I knew I would find Molly's letter. I kept looking across the room trying to see it, but one long envelope that stuck way out hid anything else. The long envelope I knew to be the account from the electric power company; they always used longer envelopes than anyone else.

As I said, I did get some homework done, but not much. There was my Dad not home, and Mum saying nothing about it, then suggesting I go away for a holiday, and that meant missing school, and then looking the queer way she did. It is no wonder some kids don't get their schoolwork done if they get mixed up the way I did. And I was frightened, and I thought if I could only read Molly's letter it might explain everything, or at least the part about my going away on holiday.

Mum came into the lounge, too, when she finished in the kitchen, and sat in the armchair: she fitted that chair; when Dad sat in it, he looked small. But she filled it all right. She started in to darn some socks, and I stared away at my books, because I knew if I looked up I would look at the writing bureau.

At last I had had it. I closed my books carefully and stacked them into my schoolbag. So help me, while I was doing it, I could hear the sound of her darning, a faint shssh as she pulled the wool up through the sock on the end of the needle, and I began to feel my eyes being dragged up to look again to the writing bureau. It was definitely time to get out before I gave the show away. Then I did look up. Sure enough, I saw the letter slot at the top of the bureau half out of the corner of my eyes, and she looked up from her darning, straight at me, and there I was prickling all over, feeling like the rear end of a dirty cow. I said the first thing that came into my head.

'Where's Dad, Mum?'

Well, it was her turn now. She didn't actually change colour, but she jumped inside, if you know what I mean.

'You don't know?' she whispered. Normally, she had a strong voice, much better than the way other women spoke; you never had any trouble hearing her.

'No,' I said, happy the way I had got out of being caught looking at the writing bureau. 'I just wondered where he was, not being home. Is he working overtime? I just thought I would ask, that's all. In case you want me to stay up with you, or anything like that.'

That last bit was bullswool of course, but I had to be careful.

She looked at me in a funny way, and for a second I thought it wasn't going to be so good after all.

'Why didn't you ask about him before, son?' she said.

'I don't know. I just didn't, I suppose.'

She half rolled up the sock she was darning, and shoved the needle in it, and sat back, and for the first time for weeks she looked soft at me. When she got soft she had a wonderful face, lighted up and friendly in a way nobody else could be friendly, able to make me feel as though everything was

66

fine and dandy, and forget all the other business, and feel good to be me.

'When I was a little girl I used to sit up with my mother and we would have wonderful times,' she said. 'She would play the piano for me, and I would dance for her. Your mother learned to dance, you know that? And I would dance to her playing the piano, and when I was tired, she would sing to me.'

She went on like that for quite a while, with all sorts of her memories, and even though I wasn't really interested in that kind of stories, it was very enjoyable, my sitting there at the table, my chin in my hand, listening to her without much attention, with a pleasant feeling like sitting in front of an open fire. I always got on with my parents when I was alone with one or the other of them.

'And did you ever dance for your father or anything?' I said to her. She half turned her face away from me, looked across to the mantelpiece, and stared at it for a while, and then said, 'No, son, I didn't.'

'I don't suppose grown-up men like dancing, it being a bit sissy,' I said, trying to get her going again, because it was obvious the wind was out of her sails.

I don't think she paid me any attention, for she stared away at the mantelpiece some more and then said, 'I only danced for my mother.'

'If I was to do anything for you, it would be to play marbles,' I said, doing my best to keep things alive. 'I know a few tricks on a bike, of course, but I haven't got one though.'

She heard me then. She looked back at me and I could see that the open-fire feeling had gone bung. I could have kicked myself for mentioning a bike, but it had slipped out quite naturally. Then I knew for certain that when Dad had gone back in the morning there had been real trouble, and I hated bikes. Yet she didn't look wild with me, I don't think; I don't know exactly how she looked at me, but I didn't like it.

Then she said, 'You are a good boy, Jimmy, to want to do something for your mother. You are a good boy.'

I knew she wasn't thinking of me in the same way that she thought of herself as a little girl, though. And she looked so big and strong in that big chair. When I slid out from behind the table, pulling my schoolbag behind me, I could feel a trembling feeling in my stomach.

As I grow up and get smarter and smarter, I better understand how my mother looked at different times. Even now, though, I can't understand her sitting there, with her arms on the sides of the chair, her darning in her lap, looking right at me as though she was trying to work out how much I weighed. So very serious, too, and the light made her face a milky colour.

I stood not knowing exactly what was going to happen next, and said, 'I wouldn't say I was so very good, but I'm not too bad, I suppose. I'm better than Molly was at my age, I daresay.'

'Mmm?' she said.

'I'm better than Molly was, I bet.'

'Oh,' she said, and her eyes lost the staring look. 'It's time you were off to bed, son. I'm very sorry.'

She said those last words quickly, as though she had stood on my toe.

'What for?' I said. 'I know it's time to go to bed. You don't have to be sorry, Mum.'

I lay in bed for I don't know how long doing my best to work things out, and my best certainly wasn't good enough. I used to think that in bed at night I was underneath a great layer of darkness thousands of miles thick, with God sitting on top. I was probably thinking about that when I heard my mother moving across the passage, snapping off the lights, and going upstairs to bed. Then I thought about the letter, and for a long time imagined or dreamed, I'm not sure which, that I was chasing Molly and hitting her over the head with the bill from the electric power company.

Then, you know, I was actually out of bed, tying my

pyjama cords tighter, standing in my bare feet on the cold floor, hardly able to see at all except for a little grey light from behind the window blind, and I was getting ready to sneak down the passage to look for Molly's letter. I was actually doing all that before the idea had entered my mind. I stood without moving for a while, then crept over to the door and opened it quietly and listened. Perhaps I was actually walking in my sleep, because I can't remember hearing a sound, not even my own feet on the floor or the door opening. I didn't seem to be even breathing. And the house was so very very quiet; even the passage floor did not squeak as I crept down to the lounge. I was seeing Molly's handwriting on the pages, and almost reading some kind of horrible nonsense she had written about me. I guided myself down the passage with the tips of my fingers brushing along one wall, really not hesitating, straining my eyes wide open, slowly seeing more and hearing, too, as if my ears were getting used to the dark: the creaks and the shivers that an old house makes during the night, and a faint sighing sound of the sea wind outside all became distinct, and by the time I had reached the door of the lounge my breath was clicking against the back of my throat, which was as dry as a bone.

I slid through the half-open door and the lounge was quite light, as the blinds were up, and there was the shine of the moon pretty well in. I didn't waste a second, though, just dived across the room to the bureau, and reached up to the top slot. There was nothing there. Except that envelope from the electricity company. Nothing. I turned round and fairly ran back to the door. I knocked hard against the big chair as I went, and tripped, sprawling on the floor with a bang. I lay there listening with my face half turned against the carpet, not really caring, all the time thinking 'no letter, no letter, no letter'. There was not a sound from upstairs, so I got to my hands and knees and crawled slowly around the door and into the passage.

There I did hear something, like the scraping of a chair against the floor. I stood up and looked down the end of the passage, and saw light coming through the half-open kitchen door, and you know, I was glad. I wasn't actually thinking, then; just standing there, holding my pyjamas, puffing a little. Then with hardly any worry, off I went down the passage. I could always say I was going to the lavatory to explain what I was doing out of bed. When I reached the door I stopped for a second. Who was in there? At first crack I had thought it must have been Dad, come home and gone into the kitchen in the short time I had been in the lounge. Now somehow I had lost my brave feeling. A burglar, with lumps of lead pipe to bash my brains out, a madman from some loony-bin; those kind of people floated in my mind. I decided that if it was anything like that I would scream blue murder, and opened my mouth and took a deep breath, so that I would have a flying start to do just that, and peeped my head around the door.

Mum was sitting at the kitchen table with her back to me, running her hands over a whole box of old photographs that she had emptied over the table. Sitting there in her blue nightdress, leaning over, flicking the photos through her hands, hardly looking at any one of them for long; flick, flick, flicking away, and wriggling on the wooden chair all the while, so that it squeaked ever so slightly. I closed my mouth shut, and my breath was all boxed up in my chest and hurt and I felt bloody awful. I could even see her bare feet tucked under the table, about ten times the size of mine, and the skin on them was brown and wrinkled, and the toes were wriggling, too. And then she started to sniff with her wriggles; as her shoulders went up each sniff became louder. I pulled back from the door and crept the first few yards back up the passage and then took jumping steps, but land-ing on my toes without a noise, until I was near my own bedroom. Then I ran in there and took a running jump into bed. Even in the dark I could take a running jump into my bed. I was pretty good in the dark, all things considered.

But I lay in bed, looking up into the layer of darkness. There was no letter from Molly, I was sure of that, because if there had been, Mum would have put it in the bureau, regardless. Each letter Molly had ever written had been put up there straight after she had read it. All letters went there, and every week or so she pulled them out and burned them, except the bills which hadn't been paid.

So I was certain there was no letter from Molly, and that Mum had been telling fibs. And after all that, she got up and got a box of old photos, all of them taken long before I was born, of her and Dad long ago, and her family when she was a kid; she got up, got that old box, and shuffled them up, and now she was crying.

And then something struck me: the light wasn't on in the kitchen when I first went up the passage, but had been turned on during the few seconds I had been in the lounge. Yet to get to the kitchen Mum had to come down the stairs, the foot of which was not far up from my bedroom door, across the other side of the passage. It frightened me to think that as I had been sneaking up the passage, she must have been not far ahead of me, going to the kitchen.

10

I never told anybody what was going on. Not a soul. I was like any other boy, and managed to keep my end up pretty well, skiting about things at home and the rest, on the odd occasion. As, for instance, when I went to Joe Waters' place for tea. That was when Joe first came to our school, after his parents had shifted to Raggleton from Albertville. He sat next to me in class. I didn't think much of him at first because he was a funny-looking coot, the way his hair stuck up and his ears stuck out, and his teeth, without actually sticking out, gave you the idea that they could if they wanted to. But I was about ten, then, and always was a good judge of character, and it didn't take me long to see that Joe Waters was one out of the bag. He was the lean type, like me—you certainly couldn't say he was skinny—and smart, too.

I said to him in the lunch hour in his first week, 'If your ears stuck out any more you could fly with them.' A bunch of us kids were sitting around in the sun, leaning against the wall of the bike shed, kicking the backs of our shoes in the dirt, and it seemed fair enough to give the new boy a going over.

Anyway, he grinned at me and said, 'If your nose turned up any more you couldn't see over the top of it.'

Everybody laughed, so I said, 'If your hair stuck up any more you would look like a fuzzy-wuzzy.'

'If you had any more freckles there wouldn't be any room left for your skin.'

That did it, of course, and we both stood up and hit each other about the same time, and kept on doing that for a while. We had similar styles and did the same things to each other, and both stopped at the same moment and sat down puffing. The other kids were disappointed, of course, and tried to get us to go on, but we weren't interested.

'If you had any bigger fists you would knock me out,' I said to Joe.

'And if you were any tougher my fists would get broken up,' said Joe.

So we both had some respect for each other at the same time, too.

He was smart in other ways. He was always the first to see my jokes, for instance. I was a pretty good joke-maker, and Joe was pretty good at laughing. Some of my jokes were over the heads of a lot of people, but never Joe. He saw them, all right. I wish I could remember some of the jokes that Joe saw when the others didn't.

Joe was also very good at predicting the weather. That's not bad for ten, if you think about it. He would sniff the air in the morning and screw up his eyes and think, and then say, 'There's rain about' or 'It'll be fine today,' and, by golly, he would nearly always be right. After he started doing this, some of the other kids reckoned that Joe was overdoing it, as he got around to using expressions you read in the weather reports. Like 'overcast with a slight drizzle developing later' or 'southerly winds moderating later in the day' and stuff like that. I admit that perhaps he was a little confused on wind directions, although that was no reflection on his weather predictions; when the wind blew from the north and he had predicted south it was just that he had got north and south mixed up, that's all. He had known where the wind was going to come from, all right.

That reminds me, the kids telling him how he was just repeating weather office expressions finally got his goat, because not long afterward Sister Angela, who had heard that Joe was a great one for predicting the weather, asked him what the weather would be the next day, when we were to have a sports afternoon. Well, Joe got up and stared out of the window, with all the class watching him. He sniffed the air, and screwed up his eyes, and thought for a long time, then turned back and said, 'Sister, it looks to me as though it will be pissing with rain.' He got the strap, of course, but as he told everybody afterwards, nobody could say he was using stuff from a weather report.

I made up my mind to tell Joe about what was going on at home after the funny business about Molly's letter. As I went to sleep I imagined myself telling Joe even about the funny marble feeling that came over me from time to time. Up next morning, though, I changed my mind; in the morning nothing seems that bad. And I remembered a lot of the whopping lies I had told Joe about my mother and father; he would have had the wood on me properly if I turned around and told him differently.

I told him the biggest lies that time I went to his place. About his second week at school he came bowling up to me and said, 'Jimmy, would you like to come to our place for tea tomorrow night?' He was wanting to be more friendly, I daresay, so I said, 'Why not? If I am allowed.' I was allowed, and so the next day after school I went home with him, after we had played around with the other kids.

He didn't live far from us—in Raggleton, of course, nobody lived far from anybody else. His father had taken over the local drapery, so they were well-off, and their house, as you would expect, was a good one: big, and two-storied, like ours, though not nearly so old. There was a nice lawn in front, with a monkey puzzle tree in the middle of it.

'The chairman of the harbour board lived here one time,' said Joe as he clicked open the gate, and held it open as if he was showing me into a palace. I noticed that their path was smooth concrete, while ours was old gravel, and it came to me that Joe was out to show off in front of me.

'Way back, y'know, a millionaire built our home,' I said right back to him. About the only thing I knew about the place, really, except for the maniac who painted the bathroom black, was that Dad had told me that an old woman with dozens of tomcats used to live there once.

I followed Joe up the path, and he opened the front door and in I went, and straight away felt the soft carpet under my feet. Green stuff that started right at the door and went all over the house, as far as I ever saw, anyway. Not all the carpet was green, I suppose, but it was all carpet.

'Home, Mum,' yelled Joe, and led me from a hallway through the lounge, which had all new-looking brown furniture in it, across a passageway, and into the kitchen. His mother was there with a frilly apron on, a big wooden spoon in her hand.

'So this is Jimmy,' she said.

'Who do you think it is?' said Joe.

I said how-do-you-do, and she shook my hand, and I felt very shy. She was so nice-looking, I was surprised. Joe being on the funny side, I expected his parents to be that way, too. In looks, I'm talking about. She was fair-headed, small, and when she smiled she had bright white teeth, and her blue eyes crinkled up, and you could well imagine she wouldn't mind playing hide-and-seek with you. And she was wearing what must have been a best dress, blue, and her hair was combed and clipped back, and she had lipstick on. Darn it, she didn't look very old at all.

As a matter of fact, I told her that, and she was tickled pink. Joe was pleased, too.

'I feel very old sometimes,' she said. 'Now that I'm thirty I am what they call halfway old, I suppose.'

'I must say you don't look as old as thirty,' I said, and that went down well, too.

She gave Joe and I a big piece of sponge cake with cream and bits of pineapple on top. And talk; honestly, she chattered away to Joe and I as though we were friends of hers. We ended up by staying in the kitchen about half an hour, telling her about school and what went on there, and she told us what she had been doing during the day, and acted out a conversation she had had with a funny butcher.

She even imitated the way the butcher talked, shaking herself around the way he did, apparently, only her chest jiggled when she shook and I bet his didn't.

Joe and I went out to play afterwards, and I could see that he was as pleased as a cat with two tails. He could see his mother had been a big success.

'She's pretty good, isn't she?' he said.

I nodded my head. Then to keep my end up, I said, 'My mother is a lot bigger than she is, and a lot stronger.'

Joe let that pass, and we had a good time till it was nearly dark, climbing the pine trees at the back of the house. His mother called us when tea was ready, and we washed up in the bathroom, which was tiled halfway up the walls. His father arrived home then, and you should have heard the racket. He kissed Joe's mother as though it was ages since he had seen her, and then kidded her about the way she was dressed up.

'Is that for me or for him?' he said, and I felt embarrassed. She laughed and pushed him in the chest, and he picked her right up off the ground and swung her around. Joe laughed his head off, and I could only stand there feeling silly. He must have twirled her around three or four times, so fast it made her petticoat show.

Then he put her down and picked Joe up and twirled him about, too. He was a hefty sort of chap, especially considering that a draper spends most of his time messing around with women's clothes. He was very dark and suntanned, and had a round, jolly face. It wasn't till after he had put Joe down that he turned to me, shoving his hand out for me to shake as though I was a man, and saying, 'You're the nipper that's a friend of Joe's, eh?' He shook my hand up and down, and said, 'Always be glad to see you, Jimmy,' giving a big wink. When I looked at him I couldn't help grinning; he had three or four lines curving around the sides of his face that made him look as if he was smiling even when he wasn't, and I could see also where Joe got his big teeth from.

It was good fun being with the three of them, at least for a while. We ate in the kitchen, talking like billy-ho, Joe's father telling us about football matches he had seen —he had actually drunk beer with some of our top footballers a couple of years before—and speed car races at Albertville. And when he did smile, those lines around his face became very deep. He reminded me of the man in the advertisement for oranges who actually looks like a smiling orange.

And then for some reason I began to feel bad-tempered, though I didn't show it. They asked me some questions about my parents, and I really let them have it: whoppers, like how my father had owned lots of race horses that won big events, and how he was wounded in the arm killing dozens of Germans in the First World War, and that my mother was a swimming champion when she was a girl. I could hear myself babbling away, with some of my words getting mixed up, and actually stuttering up together, with Joe's mother looking at me with her head on one side, smiling, and his father nodding his round head every few seconds, as though he wanted to make sure I knew he believed me. Boy, I really let them have it; I can't remember most of the lies I told.

Anyway, when I finished, Joe's mother crinkled her eyes at me and beamed, and said, 'I know one little boy who is very proud of his mother and father.'

My bad temper disappeared when I looked at her, and everything was fine for the rest of the meal. You know Joe's father was a bouncing sort. When we finished he slapped his chest and pushed his chair back and said, 'The inner man is content,' in a loud voice, stood up and picked Joe's mother right out of her chair, holding her under the armpits, and said, 'A little more polish and your cooking will be good,' and then, so help me, he put her down and slapped her on the bottom, and she gave him a hug and giggled. Joe must have noticed that I was astounded, because he spoke about it afterward, as we went upstairs to his bedroom to mess around with his meccano set. 'They're always fooling around like that. Silly, aren't they?'

'I don't know,' I said, not wanting to hurt his feelings.

'Men and women always go on like that when they're married,' he said. 'That's the way it is.'

I didn't say a word at that, letting Joe go ahead into his bedroom: quite a big room, with wooden walls, brown rugs on the green carpet, and a great big wooden chest in addition to the usual kind of furniture. Joe heaved the lid of the chest up and took out his meccano set from a whole pile of interesting-looking junk, slammed the lid down again, and turned to me. He looked a little bad-tempered himself, with his lips nearly over his teeth, and his eyes squinting a little. I looked around the room and saw a bunch of newspaper photographs of rugby players in action stuck up all over the wall. 'That's not a bad collection,' I said, wanting to keep the proceedings friendly.

'You think there is something funny about them mugging up each other like that?' Joe said, staring hard at my face. 'Don't your mother and father do it?'

'All the time,' I said. 'They go on like that every spare moment.'

'Is that right?' said Joe, leaning back against the chest.

Then off I went again: I knew they were lies I was telling, but they didn't seem that bad. I had seen a picture not long before, a sloppy one that went with a jungle feature, in which the man carried the girl up the stairs, and I tossed that in, too; only, of course, I said that my father carried my mother. That was the biggest lie, I think: the rest were just ordinary ones, such as that they were always kissing each other.

Well, this big lie rocked Joe.

'You mean he did that with one arm all shot up in the First World War?' he sort of gasped.

'It was a bit of an effort,' I said. 'He more or less had to put her over his shoulders. He is a very strong man, even though he is not so big.'

'That's not bad at all,' said Joe. He was more like his

78

old self now. 'Once, there, my father had a bath with my mother.'

It was my turn to be rocked.

'You mean in the same bath?' I said.

'Yep,' he said, with his big smile. 'I heard them. Dad came home after I had gone to bed, but I had got up to look out of the window to check up if there was going to be a frost. I heard Mum in the bath and then Dad came home in a good mood and said something about his not being able to wait—he must have been fairly grubby—and the next minute there was a heck of a splash and I went to the top of the stairs and listened a while to a swishing and swashing of water. They must have scrubbed each other.'

You know, we went on ear-bashing each other like that for the next hour or so, without even opening the meccano set, till nine o'clock came and I had to set off home. It was a Friday night, so it didn't matter my being late in bed. We talked some more about our parents, and I lied all the time when it was my turn to say anything, and then went on to other topics. I think I showed Joe some wrestling holds, too.

When it was time to go I went downstairs and said good night and thank you to Joe's parents, and they fussed over me some, and I couldn't help seeing, just by looking at them, that Joe hadn't told any lies to me. Even that bath business. Since then, of course, I've learned a lot more things about what goes on between men and women, even kings and queens, and wouldn't be surprised if it went on between Joe's parents now and then, too.

As I said, I almost decided to talk to Joe about it when everything became really bad at home, but then I remembered my whopping lies, so how could I?

I I

I woke up in the morning, after the business over Molly's letter, hardly letting myself think about the night before, and was extra careful in my washing and dressing, and did not go into the kitchen for breakfast until the very last minute, in case Mum started talking to me. I heard Dad upstairs, getting ready, and when he came down he started to sing. He had a deep voice, and when I heard him I felt that nothing could be too bad. The sun was shining, and the air was snappy, and in my clean white shirt and my blue serge shorts, with my shoes cleaned, and my hair wetted back into place, I felt as bright as a new pin. I think for a while there I was pretty well convinced I had been dreaming the night before.

In the kitchen Dad was already sitting at the table, and darn me, he looked like a new pin, too. He was wearing his good dark suit trousers and vest, and had the coat hanging from the back of his chair. He had on a clean starched white collar that made him keep screwing his neck around to settle it into place. He had that fox terrier look about him, you know: plenty of bounce, looking as though he could take the whole world on, even though he wasn't so big. He was really handsome when he dressed up, and clean-shaven, with his ears, eyes, nose, and chin all in a neat pattern, none of them trying to steal the whole show.

He grinned at me when I came in, and said, 'What ho, old chap?' Another sign that he was in a good mood.

I replied, 'Not too bad, old top,' and sat up at the table. I looked at Mum out of the corner of my eye and said, 'Hello there, Mum.' She had her back to me, leaning over the stove watching the eggs boil, and all she said was, 'Your egg won't be long, son.' She had an old brown dress on that was far too short for her, only reaching to her knees, and hanging straight from her shoulders without a belt. She had been wearing that dress for housework as long as I could remember, and the longer I could remember the worse it looked. She didn't have any stockings on and I couldn't help noticing the way the veins in the back of her legs bunched up in spots, and looked like purple lumps. I usually liked the way my mother looked, but not that morning. And again I thought of her suggesting I go away for a few days, and that didn't make her any better.

Before I had my egg, of course, I had to eat my porridge. I forgot to mention that. I wouldn't like to give the impression that I just had an egg for breakfast. I had porridge, an egg, three or four pieces of toast and marmalade, and a drink of milk. I was drinking a lot of milk, those days, not because I liked the stuff, not on your life. I wanted to build up my physique, you know, as I had an idea I might want to be a professional wrestler one day.

Eating in the morning after you are up and washed is a great thing. And after I had tucked away a fair amount I was as happy as a lark. Couldn't help it. Dad sitting there, done up to the nines, feeling good, and even Mum, though she seemed tired, certainly didn't look as though she was going to growl at anybody. She did look as though she had been dragged through a gorse bush, as they say, with her hair not done, and that old dress on, yet I could see that cooking breakfast in the morning is no time for a woman to look her best. I liked sitting in the kitchen, too, with its big cupboards and warm stove, and the old wooden walls that had friendly stains on them, and the windows behind the table that looked out on the back yard, over the sand hills and then to the sea.

'Where were you last night?' I asked Dad. That shows you how I felt—any other time I wouldn't have dared to have asked that.

'Around and about, my boy. Doing this and that. Here,

there, and everywhere.' He smiled as he spoke, and slapped his chest with his good hand.

'I just wondered, that's all, seeing you weren't home,' I said.

'You are just like your mother used to be,' he said, lifting himself up and down in his chair. As I said, he could sort of bounce when he was in the mood. 'Long ago she used to ask me where I went nights. Your father was a popular man, those days, and I had all sorts of friends.' He squiggled his neck around in his collar, and winked, and said again, 'All sorts.'

'I've got all sorts of friends, too,' I said.

'Have you got any girl friends, eh?'

I explained that there were some girls at school but that we boys didn't have much to do with them, although one or two of them sometimes had comic books that we borrowed. By and large, though, the girls were so silly, we didn't even think of them. We certainly never played with them.

'When you grow up you might change your mind,' Dad said, 'if you are a chip off the old block.'

He smiled without showing his teeth—I'm not sure exactly how you would describe the expression on his face—and looked over toward Mum. She had taken some of the plates from the table and was stacking them on the sink, and didn't seem to be listening.

'When I was a single man, lots of girls used to chase me,' he went on. 'And, by jove, I let a few of them catch me.' He slapped his hand on the table and pushed himself up and down as he spoke. 'The best years of your life, Jimmy. The best years of your life are ahead of you. And after the best years come the worst years. That's if your luck is bad. But you'll have good luck, I'll see to that. I'll see you don't have the luck I've had.'

I could see he was heading into his old story, so I slid out from behind the table, as carefully as if I was balancing a book on my head, and said, 'We haven't much time, Dad, so we had better get cracking.'

'Yes, yes,' he half-shouted, and bounced up. 'Let us be

82

away and cracking, young man, and yet, mark my words. you might have more time than you think.'

Not sure whether I liked him in such a mood—honestly, you would have thought he was at a football match, and his team was winning—I picked up my schoolbag from my bedroom, gave my face a quick rub-over in the bathroom, streaked back down to the kitchen, anxious to be out and about. Dad had gone back upstairs, and Mum was finishing clearing the table.

'All serene,' I said. 'Am I all spit and polish?' I was trying to cheer her up, you see.

She wiped her hands on a tea towel and took a deep breath as she looked at me. Even if I say it myself, I couldn't help noticing that the sight of me seemed to do her good. For a minute there, a look came across her face, as though she had suddenly thought of something cheerful. I think of her most at those times, when I was standing before her, and she looking me over, so tall and strong-looking, with sometimes a bit of a smile on her face, other times putting her hands out to hold me by the shoulders, eyeing me up and down, fixing up my collar, or making me roll up my sleeves properly; times like this morning, nearly the last morning of all, when she made me feel that nothing too bad could ever happen to me while she was around, and that she would always be there when I came home from school.

'That shirt is lasting well,' she said. 'Now keep yourself clean until Father Gilligan comes.'

Father Gilligan came to school once a week for confessions, and she was always keen on my clothes being clean for him. I pretty well always had to wear a clean white shirt, as I did this day, for his coming. It certainly made it hard after school though; a white shirt is a handicap when you want to muck around.

'It'll be as clean as when I put it on,' I told her.

I felt almost sick with wanting to tell her how I felt, and because I couldn't think of words to suit my feelings, I came up with the next-best thing.

83

'I'll go down to see Molly if you really want me to, Mum,' I said.

'I don't really want you to go,' she said quickly. So quickly that it seemed the words were right there on the tip of her tongue. 'Sometimes Mum knows what is best, that's all. But you forget all about it for a while yet. Forget all about it.'

'All right,' I said, though what she said was mixed up. She knew best, she didn't really want me to go, yet she suggested that I should go.

'And don't say a word about this to your father. Not a word.' That came out quickly, too, and louder, and I blushed, thinking of the morning before.

She gave me a peck on the forehead as Dad came back down the stairs, just bumped me with her lips, and I went back out to the passage and out the back door. Dad was standing at the top of the steps whistling. It was years since I had seen him in such a mood—when I was much younger he went on like that one night when he came home and told me he had been given a raise in wages.

'Let us go hence,' he said. The bald patch on top of his head was shining, his eyes were bright; boy, he really was feeling great. He really looked well. I decided that I liked him like that, not that he was too bad in the mornings, anyway.

'O.K., Pop, we are on our way,' I yelled, and headed down the steps ahead of him.

Then I saw it. The bike. It was leaning against the gate. A snazzy job that gave me a lift that was almost like being sick. It had a yellow framework, handle bars of silver with black rubber grips, and a slick silver headlamp, and fat balloon tyres, and the way it was leaning against the gate tilted the handle bars so that the headlamp was looking right at me. I don't want to seem silly, but that bike struck me like a bomb.

I stood there and pointed.

'Look at that, Dad.' I squeaked, being a stupid kid. As

I looked up at him and saw his face with this smile, and with his head bouncing up and down again, the old bomb exploded. I gave a yell that could be heard for miles.

'It's mine, is it?'

Now Dad started to jump on each foot, bouncing from one to the other, his bad arm swinging up and down, really dancing. Like jitterbugging, as they call it. You'd have thought somebody had given him a motorcar, the way he went on.

'That's it, boy,' he laughed. 'Yours, all yours, from Pop. Good old Pop, eh?'

Well, I did a hop, skip, and jump, then a couple of whoopees, and there the two of us were for a moment, hoofing it around in circles as though we were loony. I think I even yelled out, 'Good old Pop, good old Pop,' to show how pleased I was with him, and it was probably this that made me pull up dead in my tracks as I was about to start off up the path to grab the bike. I remembered Mum. I looked back at Dad. He was standing still now.

'Mum knows, doesn't she?'

He wrinkled his nose and replied, 'Of course.' Then he waved his hand up the path, and said, 'Off you go. I got it for you last night, if you want to know. She knows all about it. Off you go.' He was anxious to see me started. But I was a fool, a little fool, the biggest, damnedest, stupidest fool in the whole world, so glad about getting the bike, and wanting Mum to see me the first time I rode it.

I took a couple of steps back down the path and called out at the top of my voice, one of my really loud calls, 'Come out here and watch me. Come out here and watch me, Mum.'

Dad was silent, and I cocked my head and listened. All I could hear was a sound of rattling dishes.

'Go and get her, Dad,' I said. 'Please get her to come out and watch.'

He didn't budge for a second, and a lot of the bounce went out of him. Then he shrugged his shoulders and said,

'Of course, son. I'll get her to come out and watch you. Wait there.' He ducked up the steps, and even though I could see he was not too pleased, I thought it was all for the better. When the good things are happening, or look as though they might happen, a kid likes to have his parents looking. So I waited there, at the bottom of the steps, shuffling from one foot to the other—it must have looked as though I had been locked out of a lavatory—until Mum came to the door. She came to the top of the steps with Dad behind her, holding her arm.

Looking up at her, I said, 'What a bike, Mum, what a bike. I wanted you to see me take off on it. Just watch my smoke, that's all.'

'Your mother's surprised, Jimmy,' Dad cackled out from over her shoulder. 'Your mother's surprised.' He laughed like billy-ho, though it wasn't the same kind of laugh he and I had been having together.

She looked so big to me now, on top of those steps, with one hand on her waist, looking down at me; I could see that she really was surprised.

'I'm glad, Jimmy,' she said at last. 'Now off you go and I'll watch you.'

As soon as I heard her I knew she hadn't known about the bike. It was a kick in the stomach for me. One of the reasons Dad was so pleased was because it did something to her. He was grinning behind her back at me. I thought all this in a very quick way, you know, the way you think when you fall over and haven't hit the ground yet. Then I turned back up the path and saw the bike, and I stopped thinking about anything else. I mean it appealed to me, that bike, because I was at that stage when a bike meant a lot. So I ran up to the gate, with a shout, and I grabbed it by the handle bars, pulled it upright, and pushed it out the gate to the side of the road.

'It's a beaut. A real beaut,' I yelled. I thought if I made a big enough fuss Mum and Dad would forget the rest. I looked back toward them, to see if they were watching

86

me, and saw her pulling her arm from his grip. Her eyes were closed and her hair was all over the place and her face was screwed up. And she got her arm loose with such a jerk that it shot up across her face, and Dad seemed to be pulled part of the way with it, right to the top of the steps, where he wobbled back and forward. He reached out with his good arm and grabbed her by the shoulder and pulled himself back again, so that he swung hard against the wall. The heave he gave pulled her forward. She put both her arms right out in front of her face as she fell down the side of the steps to the ground. There was a scrunch as she landed on her knees and hands on the loose gravel. Right on her hands and knees with a smack. Dad kept on leaning against the wall, his face red, and his suit coat swelling in and out. She stayed there on all fours, her head down, as though she wasn't exactly sure where she was. Then she twisted her head around and looked up at me. Her eyes were wide and terribly bright, and for a moment I thought she was going to cry out and crawl up the path. But she pulled one leg under her body and pushed herself up to her feet, not taking her eyes off me, smacking her hands together. She was white as chalk. Her mouth opened and closed a few times, and all the while now she was looking at me, and then she brought her hands up to the sides of her face and pushed her hair back round the side of her head, and it seemed as her hands went back they stretched her mouth into the funniest smile she had ever given me.

'Don't be frightened, boy. It was an accident and I'm not hurt. Silly Mum slipped and fell. There's nothing to be frightened about.'

Each word came banging out as though she was putting all her might into speaking. She took a couple of steps forward and held her hands out, still with that smile. I could see her palms were red and dented where the stones had dug into them.

'Don't look so frightened, Jimmy,' she said, much louder now. 'Don't be a ninny. I'm not hurt. It was a silly old accident. I'll go back up to the top of the steps and watch you bike down the road. Off you go.'

She turned sideways to me and edged to the foot of the steps, never taking her eyes off me.

'I bet I don't fall a second time,' she said. Still with that smile.

Then I heard Dad saying, 'On your way to school, Jimmy. Get on your way now.' He was standing away from the wall now, red as a brick in the face, the shoulder of his lame arm hanging lower than the other, his mouth hanging open.

My eyes were hurting. They ached. I think I tried to blink them and I couldn't. I wanted to shut them tight and shake my head.

Mum got right back to the top of the steps, where she had been before she fell, and called, 'For goodness' sakes, Jimmy, off you go. Nothing's wrong. Off you go.' Her voice was higher. 'I can't stand here all day and watch you.'

I moved my whole head around, dropped the bike sideways so that I could get my leg over the bar, pushed off with my other foot, and then stood on the pedals. I wobbled slightly at first, but a few good shoves on the pedals and I was away.

I can remember doing all that, as though it happened a minute ago, yet I can't remember what I shouted. Because as I took off I shouted something over my shoulder to them. I can even remember the shout was so hard it twisted my throat, and sort of shook my eyes loose. I couldn't see much at first, but the rush of air as I picked up speed cleared my eyes, even though they still hurt.

12

DID I tell you this was the day the priest came? Father Gilligan, tall as billy-ho, as high as a telegraph pole. One of the girls in the primer classes burst into tears the first time she saw him. He had to duck slightly to come through a door, and when he stood at the top of the classroom to give us the old stuff about God and the Virgin Mary, how much Jesus loved us, venial and mortal sins and all that, he was about a foot higher than the blackboard. A smallish head and a big beaked nose like a hen's beak. We asked Sister Angela about his nose once and she said it was a Roman nose, and if we asked any more questions like that we would have to confess it to him the next time he came. That shut us up. He wasn't funny-looking, though he might sound like that: he was thinnish, of course, with big hands and feet, and small round eyes, which didn't help his Roman nose and great height, yet dressed in black and holding himself straight he was pretty impressive.

He had a deep rough voice, and was always the same: that is, he didn't do his block about sin, the way some priests do. Once, there, Sister Angela had given a long pep talk about pride, how it was a sin to go around thinking you were the cat's pyjamas, so the next time I went to confession I confessed that for about three or four days I had been full of pride about the fact that I had beaten the other kids in a competition to see who could piddle the highest up the lavatory wall. I won by about two feet, nearly getting it up to the roof. Well, Father Gilligan did snort rather queerly over this, but he certainly didn't do his block. On the other hand, that priest I told about my sometimes thinking God was a bastard nearly tipped the confessional over in his excitement.

So my blowing my top this day should not be taken as a smack at Father Gilligan. As far as priests go, he was one of the best. I don't blame it on him. He and his kind are the in-between men, I think, and my quarrel is with God. Here I was pedalling my new bike down the road, a chance in a million for someone like God to step in and give me a helping hand. One of his right-hand men, you might say, was going to be around, and here was his chance to operate. It's all very well to pull off a few miracles now and then, by having people go all the way the heck over to France and dunk themselves into the water at Lourdes, or to make the bread and fishes go a whole lot further; it's all very well to cut up those capers in front of the grandstand, as it were, but if he is such a hot scone why doesn't he do more day-to-day stuff?

Not that I care. It's the way it strikes me, that's all. Because that morning, heading down the road—all right, I was snivelling a bit at the time—I did think of Father Gilligan, about his coming that day, and that gave me a way ahead. I might even tell him, I remember saying to myself, 'I'll tell him, I'll tell him.' I actually said it out loud.

When I got to the intersection I slowed down, and turned up Victoria Street on my way to school. One big sniff and an almighty spit and I was cleared up inside my head, although I still felt tight around the forehead. I sat back on the bike and took a deep breath and held it a while. Then I blew it out with a whoosh. I repeated this three or four times, and felt better, even in my eyes. That didn't mean I felt good. Just better.

You know, I can actually close my eyes and see myself as I was two years ago. I'm going on fourteen now, yet I look back on myself then as though it was a million years away, or as if it was somebody else altogether. I can see myself in my mind, just as I see Joe Waters and Sniffy Peters and the rest. I feel almost as I look back at myself then that I'm living two lives at once.

For instance, I can see myself riding this bike for the first time. Often at night I am half asleep watching myself, and I want to call out and say, 'It's all right Jimmy. We'll get even one day.' I feel so sorry for the boy I see, and almost throb with wanting to jump in there beside him to give him some help. Yet it's me I'm looking at.

Look at me, in my blue pants and white shirt open at the neck, not exactly thin but lean, pedalling away on that bike with legs that could do with a bit more meat on them, with socks up to my knees, and my dark hair shining with the water I had used to swish it back. My arms are stiff out to the handle bars, the sleeves of my shirt buttoned at the wrist, making me look sissy, and I'm staring straight down into the road as though I'm scared I'm about to fall off the bike. I've got a screwed-up, freckly, saucer-eyed look and my mouth is wriggling as if it is trying to jump off my face. What I'm doing is trying not to bawl.

I see myself like that, I suppose, because I have changed such a great deal. But it is funny. Perhaps all my life I'll be able to see me on that bike that morning. Not that it matters.

Anyway, I didn't bawl. I didn't even have to use any kind of protection trick. The bike made a difference. It was new to me and of course I had to pay some attention to how it went. The handle bars were stiff, but apart from that it seemed a very fine machine, and I made up my mind to really make the other kids sit up and take some notice. There was no other bike at school that had a yellow framework, so that was something. And then I looked around, at the houses I passed. The sun was hitting the corrugated iron roofs, there were odd voices talking, and doors banging, and on the footpath on the other side of the road were a bunch of kids from some of the primer classes wandering along to school. A tough-looking old rooster passed me going the other way. He was riding a woman's bike and I looked right at him to let him know what a stupid fool he was. He probably worked on the wharves, the way he was dressed in dirty old clothes, and the sight of him made me lose my temper and I yelled 'Yah, yah, you are an old woman.' He looked over his shoulder at me and grinned, and that made me feel ashamed of myself. Why the heck I had lost my temper I don't know. I was working up to the performance I was going to give later that day, I suppose. I had forgotten about God at the moment, too, otherwise I would have given him the works instead of some old wharfie.

It was one of those good mornings, what with the sun and the kick in the air, so when Legs Hope came zooming up from behind me I must have seemed normal enough because he didn't notice any difference in me.

'That yours?' he said, looking at my bike. Legs had had his bike a couple of years, and his knees came right up past his handle bars as he pedalled. That shows you how much he had grown in that time.

'That's right,' I said. 'The very latest. My father says it is the best bike money can buy.'

Legs rode right alongside me in order to get a close look, and on the slight turn he had to make, one of his handle bars caught his knee. His bike leapt as the front wheel skidded and he flopped sideways off the seat and the next second he and his machine were bang on the road in a beautiful gutzer. I pulled up a few yards ahead and looked back. It was the best thing that could have happened to me, seeing Legs all tangled up in his bike. I mean I forgot about everything else for the time being.

He wasn't hurt, of course. He stood up and dragged his bike with him, gave it a couple of kicks, and was back on in a jiffy. He rode on, and his monkey face was serious.

'I'll have to hit my old man up for a new bike,' he said. 'I'm getting too big for a boy's bike. What I need'—and he looked darned pleased with himself as he said this—'what I need is a man's bike. I can't be riding these toys all my life.'

Well, Legs was the same age as myself, and I could tell that what he said was supposed to be a smack in the eye for me, as his bike was the same size as mine.

'It's your legs, not the bike.'

No sooner had I said that when he swerved out to the middle of the road and the front wheel of his bike bounced into a pothole and the back wheel slid in some loose gravel. Down he went again in another beautiful gutzer. There was a clutter and yell from Legs and he turned right over on the road with the bike on top of him. He thrashed around in an awful rage, the bike wheels spinning in mid-air and his legs waving like long peasticks. I stopped again and watched him as he pulled himself out from underneath, jerked his bike up, gave it a couple more kicks, and dusted himself off. His face was red as a beetroot and he was puffing.

I didn't laugh as much as I could have, though I managed a fair amount of giggling.

'I'd like to be around when you try to ride a man's bike,' I told him.

Well, he simply squealed as he jumped on his bike. 'I'll show you, Sullivan,' he shouted. 'I'll mow you down. I'll run you down and kill you.'

I took off with a couple of yards start on him, as I saw that he was going to try to crash his bike into mine. I had to stand up on the pedals and pump my legs like a madman to keep ahead of him. Legs was a tough customer when he was worked up, and he wouldn't have cared if he had smashed both our bikes to smithereens. Over my shoulder I saw his knees absolutely jumping up and down behind his handle bars so fast they were only a bony blur, and he was leaning between them glaring at me. I really understood how he felt, his pride having taken a knock. Anyway, he chased me all the way to school, and rather than stop at the gates I kept right on going, steering around a bunch of kids, and on to the playground. Legs followed. The grass slowed us down, yet our speed was still cracking as we reached the end of the playground and I cut off to the left behind the school building and back down the other side. We must have circled the school two or three times, and though I was some distance ahead of him now, I was beginning to worry whether Legs would ever give up chasing me.

Then, passing the front of the school again I heard a loud voice I recognised, and there, on the front steps, was Sister Angela, with a wild face. I jammed on my brakes. Legs came around from the side of the building going like fury. He saw Sister standing there and, a funny thing, he never did take his eyes off her. She looked at him and he looked right back as though he had suddenly gone off into a trance or something. He didn't finish his turn around the corner. He kept on going on, not even slowing down, till he and the bike disappeared into the hedge. The last I saw of him he was still goggling at Sister. Then came a tearing and wrenching, and the hedge shook for a couple of hundred yards along the roadside, as though it had been hit by a truck, and then there was complete silence. Legs had simply disappeared, that's all. Except for a few broken twigs and one or two leaves drifting around in the air, you couldn't even see where he had been. He didn't make a sound. I knew he must be just lying there in the middle of the hedge with his bike wondering how the blazes he was going to explain it all away.

'Are you all right?' Sister Angela called out.

'Oh, yes, Sister,' said Legs from out of the hedge. 'Quite all right, thank you.'

Then she turned to me and said, 'Jimmy Sullivan, you help him out of there, tidy up the hedge after you, and the both of you will stay in after school for half an hour.'

So that was that. I hauled Legs out of the hedge and then we both pulled his bike out. He had a few harmless scratches on his face that didn't bleed much, and a cut on his knee that wasn't much, either. The bike had a buckled front mudguard which we straightened out in no time. All the steam was out of Legs, of course. He recalled that his mother often said that there were some days when you wish you had never got out of bed, and he supposed it was a day like that for him.

You know, in all the rush and excitement, it wasn't until he said those words that I thought of my day.

'Shut your silly mouth,' I crabbed at him. 'If you weren't so darn loony we wouldn't have to stay in after school.'

I mean, what the heck had he to complain about when the worst thing that happened to him in a day was to fall off his bike? I was back again to the way I felt when I saw that old wharfie riding down the street. I gave old Legs a proper telling off, and if he hadn't been so messed around by his previous experiences I daresay we would have ended up by having a fight.

13

THE day of Father Gilligan's coming—he usually came on a Tuesday afternoon—was always a good day, mainly because it put Sister Angela in a good mood. Any other day, for instance, she would have strapped Legs and me for racing around the school on our bikes.

It was the most religious time of my life, that morning, for even though I had already said a few nasty words about God, I still had a tremendous amount of time for him. Time and time again in the schoolroom I looked across to his picture on the wall, the one that showed him with a pained look on his face, with a bleeding heart painted on his chest. I knew exactly how he felt. I looked so often at that painting, and thought so much about my parents, that I started to see Mum on her hands and knees on the path after falling from the steps, and Dad panting away back against the wall. I saw them as they had been, only now God was standing near by watching them, one hand clutching at his bleeding heart.

The other kids were sitting in the room scratching away at their books; I couldn't help wondering what they would think if I told them that God had more or less put in an appearance at my place. He was dressed in a white robe that came all the way to the ground, covering his feet, and his right hand, with shining fingers, was across a red patch on his chest— I knew at once his bleeding heart was there— while his other hand was half raised at his side. He had jet-black hair that came to his shoulders in ringlets, and a face that was as white as the foam of the sea. His head was bowed and he was staring toward my parents with the saddest eyes, the way a spaniel can look when it is unhappy.

When I saw him there I covered my face with my hands. It came to me that God had been present all the time at home that morning, and I was only seeing him now because I had been looking back so hard.

I bubbled up all over the place then. The morning sun was coming in the window touching one of the two blackboards on their easels at the top of the classroom, the flowers in the vase on Sister Angela's desk were yellow and fresh, the walls with their holy pictures and road safety posters looked darned well, and even the little shuffling and squeaking noises the other kids made as they worked were as good as, say, mouth-organ playing. I was filled with feelings for God and all his angels and the Pope away in Rome, and priests and sisters, and saints and martyrs. I actually felt like praying, getting down on my knees and praying. Because if God was looking in on Mum and Dad, everything would soon be fixed up.

Sister Angela must have noticed something about me, because when the lunch hour came she called me back.

'I want to talk with you, Jimmy,' she said. She was sitting with her hands clasped together and resting on the table in front of her, looking so gentle and quiet. Sister Angela didn't look like a cat, but she reminded me of one in many ways. A cat sitting on a window ledge in the sun.

I was almost out of the door when she called me. I went back down to her table, between the rows of desks, feeling as though it was quite the normal thing for her and I to be getting together in our lunch hour. I was feeling so darned religious that I felt like her brother.

She pushed her veil back from each side of her neck with her hand, the one with a wedding ring that showed she was married to God, then clasped her hands together again.

'Sit down, Jimmy.' She almost whispered that, and I lowered myself down into the chair at the other side of her table, very slowly because I was frightened of making a noise, too. I was feeling reverent, wondering if she could tell that I had been seeing God.

97

'How are you feeling, Jimmy?' she whispered. 'I've been thinking you mightn't be very well lately.'

She had brown eyes and a clear skin, and with the sun brightening the air in the room, her smooth round face seemed to be glowing. As soon as she spoke a wonderful drowsy feeling came over me.

'I'm fine, Sister Angela. I'm fine,' I said.

'Well, Jimmy, you have always been top of the class and a good child of God. And I asked how you felt just in case you were not yourself in body, because you are certainly not yourself in spirit, child. I want you to examine your conscience very closely before you go to confession today.'

I nodded my head.

'I've been watching you lately, Jimmy, and sometimes I have not liked what I have seen. There is a God in Heaven and a Devil in Hell and there is a constant battle going on for the possession of our immortal souls. The Devil fights to get the souls of little boys, too, you know, so that he can take them down to Hell and keep them there forever and forever.'

She sat there and talked about the Devil for a while longer, still looking at me the way a cat does, not blinking, and I was feeling warm and half asleep.

'Sometimes the Devil peers out of your eyes for other people to see, Jimmy. Sometimes the Devil takes possession of a person and makes that person neglect his work and get into mischief. The Devil makes you commit little sins, till you don't think any more about it, and then the Devil makes you do bigger and bigger sins until you have no conscience left to call on God. The Devil hates a clever little boy doing well at school, and he tries to make him neglect his lessons. The Devil hates to see a good child of God not getting into mischief, so he tries to make him a bad boy of his own, who gets into all kinds of mischief.'

'Yes, Sister,' I said, for the first time seeing that she wasn't altogether pleased with me.

'Yes, Jimmy. You are not the good boy you used to be last year, I am thinking. You are not the nice little boy that came to this school when you were six years old. Each year you have drifted a little further away from God, and now these last few weeks, what a worry to me you have been.'

Honestly, you could have knocked me over with a feather. Here I was so full of religion it was nearly coming out of my ears, and up comes Sister Angela with talk like that. I sat right up in my chair and folded my arms around my chest to stop from blowing up on the spot. Sister kept on staring at me, no longer talking, and I chased around for something to say.

'I'm a God boy, Sister,' I said. 'You don't have to worry about me, I'm a God boy.'

Now where that came from I don't know. My old brain was whirling around and I wanted to hit back at her. Open went my mouth and the first time I heard myself say those words I didn't know what I meant. I saw her blink a few times, rock back in her seat, unclasp her hands, and lay them flat on the table. That cat look vamoosed, too.

'Yes, Sister,' I repeated. 'I'm a God boy. You don't have to worry a scrap.'

By this time I felt I knew what I meant, so I took a deep breath and waited for her to ask me.

'Mercy me,' she said. 'You are a one, Jimmy Sullivan. May the good Lord see you mean no harm.'

'Would you like me to tell you what I mean?' I asked her.

Really, I wanted to come right out and tell her that I was right in there with her on God's side, and even explain to her how he had come around to my place. It was obvious, even to me at my age, that she wasn't on top of her subject any longer. The old cat was off the window ledge and being barked at by a dog.

'I knew the Devil was getting into you, Jimmy,' she said. 'My goodness, saying the Holy Name in such a fashion. You haven't been paying attention in class, you've been very sullen and resentful, you've been getting into mischief, and now you are starting to take the Holy Name in vain.'

'Gosh, Sister, I haven't said anything wrong,' I said, trying to settle her down. She was looking quite flustered, and her cheeks were red. 'I've been trying to explain to you, like, that you don't have to worry about me because . . .'

'Now, Jimmy' she jumped at me, 'don't say it again like the way you said it before. It was not exactly what you said that was so bad, it was the way you said it. With such a strange look, indeed.'

'Honestly, Sister, I might have been excited, that's all,' I said. 'I didn't mean anything but good. I've never left so holy in my life as I feel today. I didn't mean to look strange.'

That fixed her. She clasped her hands again and put them against her mouth and calmed down straight away. She was a fairly young sister, so I suppose she was inclined to be on the lookout for the Devil even when he wasn't around.

Anyway, she tossed off a medium-sized sigh and went back to her old whisper. 'All right, Jimmy,' she said, 'tell me what you meant.'

I took off like a shot. 'I didn't know what I meant till I said it, Sister. But what I meant came afterwards and I could see that it was nothing for you to be worried about. Now being a God boy, that means you are a boy that God has his eye on, that's all. Like the captain of a football team who sees somebody that might fit into the team pretty well. He doesn't let on at first, and even makes the going tough for the boy he's got his eye on, but sooner or later shows that you are sorted out. No matter what happens then, there's nothing really to be worried about, because God is watching and will fix things up. The boy could really argue with God—get annoyed with him, too—that would be all right. I suppose there are a lot of people around who are God people, you might say, and girls, too, God girls, that is. You were a God girl I bet when you were going to school, Sister.'

That was the loopy stuff I spouted at her. As I said, religion was coming out of my ears. Sister Angela listened me out and slowly shook her head when I finally had to stop for a deep breath, instead of taking a lot of little ones every few words.

'That's enough, Jimmy, that's enough,' she said. 'Don't get excited again. I am so happy that you mean well, but sometimes the Devil is very clever and leads us into bad habits when we mean well. Are you getting plenty of exercise?'

I said I was.

'You are a good footballer, aren't you?' she went on. 'You can run very fast and that's a help when you play football, isn't it? And you can also take kicks, can't you?'

Sister Angela had refereed some of the seven-a-side games we played. That's how she knew, but what surprised me was her changing the subject like that.

'You're a pretty good ref, Sister.' I said. I was disappointed in this kind of talk until it struck me that she must have felt ashamed of herself for what she had said about me, and was wanting to be friends again.

'You ought to practise running,' she went on. 'When you get on to a secondary school and into big sports you will win some races, I'm sure.'

'Thanks very much,' I said.

'And when summer comes you'll go swimming a lot and play tennis, I suppose,' she said. 'I think you would be very good at those sports, too.'

'Thanks, Sister,' I said.

'What kind of books do you read? You mustn't read too much, when you are young, otherwise you will wear out your eyes, Jimmy.'

'Oh, I don't read much,' I said. 'A few comic books and some adventure and space-travel stuff, and my eyes never get sore.'

'If I were you, I would concentrate on sport, Jimmy. You are doing very well in school, so don't worry about your schoolwork; go along as you are going now, and don't worry. I'm very satisfied with your progress in school. I

101

would like to see you put more effort into sport because I think you could do well.'

That was about how we ended up, then, Sister Angela and I. I had really hit her for a six and made her change her tune properly. She talked on about sport for a while longer, with nothing more about the Devil getting his hands on me. She actually got up and walked to the door with me after we had finished, putting a hand on my shoulder.

The rosary beads at her belt jingled and her black robes had a camphor smell as I brushed against her, and again I filled up with religion, and was almost going to tell her about God showing himself to me. But I was hungry, and I thought it would mean we would get into another conversation that would last even longer than the last one, and already about ten minutes of my lunch hour had gone. Perhaps, though, if I had told her it would have saved me from blowing up later.

Anyway, she stood at the door and said, 'Tell your mother I would like to see her soon, Jimmy. I want to see all mothers once a year, and I haven't seen her yet. Tell her I would like to see her about now, would you?'

As a matter of fact, Sister Angela did see the mothers every so often, so that didn't worry me. She never put kids in bad with their parents.

It was funny her mentioning that, as it turned out; she was going to see my mother sooner than either of us dreamed of, without my having to tell Mum, either.

14

FATHER GILLIGAN came into the classroom that afternoon, pecking his beak nose in our direction in a sort of bow, and smiling as though he wasn't expecting much in the way of sins today. There were fourteen of us in the class, and we all had to go to confession, so it was a wonder that he didn't sometimes get down in the mouth about what he was going to hear.

As soon as I laid eyes on him the religion leaked out of me. I had had it all worked out that I was going to tell him about my mother and father down to the last detail, giving a blow-by-blow account, as they say about boxing matches, and lead up to this morning with God turning up near the foot of the steps. I had imagined him getting so interested that he would be cupping his ear with his hand and leaning his head against the grill of the confessional so that he wouldn't miss a word. What exactly he would say, I couldn't imagine, but I felt sure that as soon as I had actually got everything off my chest I wouldn't have to worry any more. What with God and one of his priests on the job, there shouldn't be a darned thing for me to get into a sweat about. My actually seeing God would put me in big with Father Gilligan, too, I imagined. From then on I would be the white-haired boy of the Church, probably turning out to be a cracking-good saint or even a martyr. If I had my choice, I thought, I would choose to be a saint, as I would already have had my share of the rough stuff. It would be a bit too much to ask of me to go off to die a martyr's death—being tickled to death by Chinese, for instance—after the iffy business at home.

Anyway, Father Gilligan arrived and put an end to all that. One look at him and my stomach rumbled. So big and black in his suit, and even though he smiled away I knew it would be one heck of a job to get down to brass tacks.

I even started to stutter and stammer in my mind as I thought of trying to tell him about Mum and Dad. As he stood at the top of the class talking to us, dishing out the usual stuff, I suppose (I couldn't hear what he was saying), I looked at him and imagined his forehead wrinkled and frowning, and his eyes glaring as he gave me a dressing down for telling terrible tales on my parents.

He had a nice face, with that big nose and blue eyes that jumped around with lights, the long jaw that moved from side to side as he spoke, and his grey hair all fuzzed up as though he didn't bother with sissy hair oil and combs and brushes. But I became so frightened I thought of his jaw and his nose bunched up with his mouth twisted to one side, and his eyes bulging as he told me off for being so bad. It came to me that perhaps Sister Angela was right when she first spoke about my slipping into the hands of the Devil.

As one of the older boys I would be one of the first to go into confession, and I could see all the rest of the kids waiting their turn outside as Father Gilligan was being stuck into me, the time slipping by, until everybody knew that I must have committed some whoppers to have been in there so long. Sister Angela would be worried and start wondering what I had been up to that she didn't know about.

I tell you, I worked myself up into a fine state. I closed my eyes and looked again to see if God was still at the foot of the steps watching after my mother had fallen to the path, but it didn't help; God was still there, at least a long-haired man in a white robe was, but when I concentrated on him he faded and changed until it looked as though he was about to turn into the Devil. I opened my eyes wide and felt my heart hitting out in my chest and for a flash I became cold, almost as if the marble feeling was going to come. What a fuss there would have been if I had had to get up from my

104

desk and rush out and rinse myself in hot water. It all passed, though, and there I was, as flat as a pancake.

Sister Angela picked out Joseph Kane and me to shift the confessional box to its usual place in the cloakroom, a few feet out from the window. I suppose it was there to put the priest with the light behind him so that he could see more of what was going on. With the doors closed, the cloakroom was a dim place, as the electric light was never turned on and that left this one small window to let in light. But I daresay it would be much harder going into confession if you had to do it in a strong light.

Well, as Joseph and I hauled the confessional—it was like a sawn-off telephone box, open each side and with a grill partition in the middle, painted a dark brown colour—I even thought of pretending to be sick so that I would be excused from going to confession. As I was actually feeling rotten, it would not have been much trouble. My insides were more churned up than the time about a year before when I had to confess that I had tasted meat on a Friday to find out if it tasted any different. Father Gilligan had been very decent about that, incidentally, and asked me if I thought it had tasted different. I said no, and he said it was very level-headed of me to realize that. He dished out a hefty load of penance, but I got off much more lightly than I had expected.

We finished getting the box right, and Joseph Kane, a fat Syrian boy whose father managed the hotel in Raggleton, pulled my arm and scared the daylights out of me when he said, 'You'll have to tell, too, y'know.'

I jumped around and almost shouted at him, 'Tell what?'

Joseph flopped his cheeks as he shook his head at me— he was a silly coot with a voice like a girl's—and made squeaky shushing noises. He whispered, 'Don't get ratty. Joe told his father and he said it was wrong. Joe's going to confess, so we all better had.'

It was so silly I felt like leaning back against the cloakroom wall and having a good laugh. The Saturday before, a bunch of us kids had been down at the beach and we had all peered through a hole in the back wall of the women's dressing sheds.

'There never was anybody in there,' I giggled.

'There might have been, y'know,' said Joseph, the pious pumpkin.

'But it's still winter, stupid,' I said. 'Everybody knows there's no swimming and we knew there wouldn't be anybody in the shed. You would have run a mile if you thought there had been someone within a million miles of the place.'

Joseph shook his head and said, 'There might have been, and I'm going to confess,' and waddled off back into the classroom. I wouldn't mind betting, now that I think about it, that looking through that hole might have been the worst sin in Joseph's life. I followed him and gave him a jab in his fat back to show him what a darn fool I thought he was.

Father Gilligan went into the cloakroom and closed the door behind him, and we all knelt in line getting ready to head on in after him one by one. I decided not to be sick, and to confess a few sins I would think up as I went along; also, I thought it was possible that I might change suddenly and be able to tell what was really worrying me. I was third in the line, and the other two went in and out like shots. Joseph, who was ahead of me, came out with his hands peaked up under his chin, and looking at the floor with half-closed eyes as if a terrible load had been lifted off his shoulders, while Barney Dawson, the oldest boy in the class, showed off by winking at us as he closed the door behind him.

I went in as quickly as I could, being careful to let the others see I wasn't too happy, but as soon as I was alone in the cloakroom and had knelt into the confessional and said the 'Bless me, Father, I have sinned,' I lost control.

I remember Father Gilligan saying, 'Speak up, m'boy, I can't hear you,' but I could only flop around for a while until I became desperate and invented sins right and left. I remember saying that I had taken two apples without my mother's permission, told five or six lies, missed saying my prayers, taken the Lord's name in vain—I suppose that would be true—disobeyed my father twice, been cruel to animals, thrown stones at little girls, and looked into a dressing shed where five or six women were taking their clothes off.

As I ran on with deeds like that I peered through the grill to see how it was going over. All I could see was the edges of Father Gilligan's face against the light of the window. He had been staring out the window at the playground, I felt sure, but his whole head shifted around as I looked.

'Did you say five or six women?' he asked.

I dropped my eyes and hummed and hawed about there must have been a lot of women in the sheds once, although there were none when I had done my looking.

'That's different,' he said. 'Quite different.' I looked back up and saw his head swing around to the window again—as he turned his nose came more and more into view until it was sticking out from the shape of his head like a big shadow.

'You've had a busy week, m'boy,' he said. 'Are you sure you have had time to have done what you say you've done?'

'I suppose I've been worse than usual and got through a lot more sins,' I said.

Father Gilligan said, 'Hmm,' in a drawn-out way. In case he thought I might be exaggerating, I gave him something else to think about by saying, 'I've been bearing false witnesses against my neighbours, as well.'

'What neighbours?'

'People around and about,' I replied, hoping he wouldn't ask me their names, because at the moment I wouldn't have a chance of thinking of any.

'What have you been saying about them, boy?' The way he spoke made it plain that he was interested.

'I made up tales about them,' I said. 'I say things about them that aren't true. I make things up about them.'

107

'What sort of things?'

I tried hard to think of an untruth about somebody but I couldn't, so I told him that I had forgotten exactly what it was I had been saying.

'To make a good confession, m'boy, it is not necessary to have committed a lot of sins,' said Father Gilligan. 'Boys are not expected to have offended God a great deal, so you must not worry if, when the time comes to go to confession, there is little that you have on your conscience.'

'Yes, Father,' I said.

'Is there anything else you want to tell me?'

I screwed my eyes up tight and heard the voices of my father and mother, shouting, and saw her on her hands and knees, looking at me, almost as though she was going to start crawling up the path. My head hurt with an awful ache and my whole body began to feel swollen. I had to open my mouth and say it, and all that force inside me sounded in the stupid whisper, 'My parents hate each other.'

'Speak up, m'boy, I can't hear you.' Father Gilligan was fed up, and after all my effort he hadn't even heard. And I couldn't say it again, so I knelt there, holding my eyes closed.

'What did you say about your parents?'

That was it, you see. I had cooked my goose with all the blithering beforehand, and now he was getting wild.

'Nothing,' I blurted, 'except that they sometimes argue with each other.'

'Oh,' he said. 'Really, m'boy, that is no concern of yours. Boys have their little arguments, don't they? So do grownups. All families have their little arguments. It is part of being in a family. Is there anything else?'

I said no, and dropped my face into my hands and listened to Father Gilligan mumble in Latin, and I was frightened again, knowing that my having seen God that morning was only my stupid imagination. Everything was going to be as bad as it had ever been.

15

'WHAT'S eating you?' asked Joe.

'Nothing,' I said

It was after school, the weather was nippy and clear and the kids were yelling and dancing around; you know how it is when school is out.

'Let's go and have gangster fights in the plantation,' said Legs, and everybody thought that was a great idea.

'I'm off home—I don't feel like it,' I said.

'Don't be dopey,' said Joe, 'Come on, it's too early to go home and it's a good day for gangster fights.'

'I just don't feel like it.'

'You might be on the losing side,' yelled Legs. 'Scared I might give you a thumping for this morning, aren't you?'

He knew darned well he couldn't give me a thumping; he was trying to make me feel so nasty that I would join in the game to prove it.

'I'm off,' I said, and walked away. Everybody called out 'scared', but I didn't mind. It was a compliment to me, in a way, as they really needed me for the gangster wars; I always had to do the organizing at those affairs.

I was about a couple of hundred yards down the road before I remembered that I had left my bike in the shed at school. I stopped and would have gone back, but the thought of getting mixed up with the others stopped me: anyway, I didn't really care if I never saw that bike again. So I decided to come back later when all the others had gone, and fill in time meanwhile by mooching around.

Joe was right, of course; there was something eating me. And I began to lose my temper in a way that was new to me. Dad and Mum fighting on the steps, getting off my rocker about religion, and kidding myself that God had actually appeared and was going to fix it all up, making a fool of myself with Father Gilligan: I thought of these things one by one and became more and more worked up. I tried to think of a decent thing that was left for me and, of course, couldn't. There wasn't a blasted thing, and I realized that for the first time in my life.

I reached the intersection and looked up the road to home. The house looked silent and unfriendly away at the far end of the road, the lupines and marram grass were flat and dead-looking about, and even the sound of the sea was heavy and numb, as though my ears were blocked.

I picked up a stone and threw it with all my might in the air. It smacked into a post as it fell. Without having any set ideas or plans I stooped down and picked up enough stones to fill both pockets.

The township was at the turn-off to the left, and I took off in that direction. Starting from a few hundred yards from the post office, the road was paved all the way through the shopping area. Not many places the size of Raggleton have their main street paved, I bet.

I saw an old man working in a flower garden in front of his house on the other side of the road. He was bent over, digging away like nobody's business, when the stone I threw missed him by a couple of feet and swished into a rosebush. He must have been deaf, because he didn't look up.

I was going to let him have some more, when farther down on my side of the road I saw a woman watching me. She was fairly old and thick, with white hair and glasses without rims, a brown scarf around her neck, and she was leaning over the front gate of a posh house, with her head cocked to one side, like a bird that is listening. I had never seen her before, but in a town the size of Raggleton you haven't a chance of knowing everybody. I stood still anyway and stared right back at her until she looked away. Then I shoved both hands in my pocket and walked her way. I kept looking at her as I got closer, knowing she would look back at me again.

110

She waited until I was level with her gate and as she turned her old nut to have a good squint at me she said, 'Did I see you throw a stone at that man in the garden?'

I kept on staring at her without even blinking for a few seconds, absolutely hating her.

'You spying on me?' I said, feeling as tough as old boots.

'No, young man,' she said. 'I'm an old lady with nothing to do sometimes except lean on a gate and look up and down the street. I hate to see little boys be naughty in my street.'

'Would you like to have your face bashed in?' I asked her. That set her back a few pegs, for she plunked her blue-and-white old hand up to her cheek and popped her eyes open wide.

'My goodness, that is absolutely terrible of you, young man. What on earth made you say that? Would you like your mummy to know what you said?'

'I don't care who knows,' I told her. 'Would you like your silly face bashed in?'

'I'm an old woman,' she said, starting to puff, 'but I can still give naughty little boys a thrashing. If your mummy and daddy knew the way you were carrying on they would give you the biggest thrashing of your young life. Are you a boy from the convent school?'

'None of your business,' I said. 'Would you like your head bashed in, too? I could bash your face and head in.'

She stood back from the gate, white about the gills, and her eyes popping. As I said, she had a thick build, and it struck me that she would be quite a handful if she got rough.

'That terrible church turning out little wretches like you,' she said. 'I'm not surprised. Go away, you little brat, or I'll call a policeman.'

Then I used a really stinking word on her, the one the other kids all reckoned was a mortal sin to use, and took one hand out of my pocket with a stone, and raised it in the air as though I was about to cut loose. She gave a scream

111

and turned around and skedaddled up the path. I waited until she was up her front steps and opening the door and then tossed the stone on to the roof. The clatter made her squeal again and then she slammed the door with an almighty bang after she got inside.

I stood waiting outside trying to decide what else I could do to her: I even considered smashing the windows of the house. Then I heard a door of the next house down opening, and a man's voice talking, so I ran on into town. That old woman was probably quite a decent stick, yet I felt great about the way I had roughed her up. I didn't give a damn whether she called the policeman, either.

I daresay that Raggleton isn't the biggest place in the world but it is a long way from being the smallest, and it was always busy, not just on Friday, either. Any day of the week you'd see two or three cars parked in the main street. Most of the shops had their corrugated iron verandahs painted a decent red or green, though there were some, I admit, that looked a bit brown and rusty. Anyway, when I got there this afternoon, the fact that there wasn't a soul to be seen in the street was unusual, but it was luck, I suppose.

I stood outside the fruit shop until I got my breath back, looking at my reflection in the window. I closed my hands into fists and bit my teeth together and kidded myself I looked like dynamite. At the back of my reflection were piles of apples, bananas, and stuff, and strings of onions hanging down from the roof. I stared so long that I got to seeing them as being dark, ugly sins in my body, smelling and dirty, but my tough face showed that I didn't give a damn. I was the toughest person in the whole world. And then inside the outline of my body a devil's face slowly took shape. It came to my chest, a dark, ugly thing with big lips that looked hot around yellow, pointed teeth, eyeing me in a friendly way, as though it had been feeding on what was inside me and was trying to show how pleased it was. I looked at the little black marks in its cheeks, the big red-hot holes of its nose, the steaming red lips and the coal-black hair, and then into its hot red-and-white eyes. Then one of the eyes winked.

I shoved one hand into my pocket and screamed, 'Keep away from me.'

In one grab my hand got a couple of stones and I threw them with all my might into the middle of the face. The window glass crashed around like an explosion and the face twisted up and the mouth stretched wide open, and in all the noise somebody else screamed, too. I turned and ran on down the street, a funny voice behind me started to yell, 'Help me, help me,' and a man bumped against me outside the barber's shop as he came running out. I kept going, hearing all sorts of noises, until a couple of hands caught me by the shoulder as I smacked right into a man's stomach.

'What's the hurry, young fellow-me-lad,' a voice I knew said. I looked up and there was Joe Waters's father grinning down at me. He was in his shirt sleeves, and he looked as though he could take care of anything.

'There's been an accident up the road. I was scared,' I said.

'So that's what all the commotion is about,' he said, and let me go. 'Well, don't be frightened, it won't be too bad. Somebody fall off a bike, eh?'

'In a window, I think.'

He looked so big, with his strong-looking chest and belly, that even though he had fancy silver clips around his shirt sleeves and a gold pin shoved into his tie, I felt like hanging on to his leg and asking him to take me home.

'If there's a bit of blood about, it's no place for a little boy,' he said. 'Off you go then, Jimmy, and I'll wander up and have a look-see. Not often we get any excitement in this place. Never seen so many people in the street except on a Friday night.'

He patted my head, and ambled off; he really hadn't paid me much attention at all, he was so curious about what was going on up the way.

113

I went on down the street until I was at the other side of the town, at the corner where the war memorial stood. The shops ended there and so did the paved street. Across the way was a bit of a park, and on past there, down the metal road and across the railway lines, was the wharf.

The war memorial was a hunk of stone with a huge statue of a soldier carrying a bayonet standing on top, looking as though he could lick the whole world. I sat down with my back against the stone, and by sticking my neck out and peering up the street I could see a bunch of people standing outside the fruit shop; Joe's father was in the middle of them now, along with the postmaster, the chap from the fish-and-chip shop, the barber, and two or three women. Then blow me if Dr Hutchinson, who came to school and looked all the kids over twice a year for the Health Department, didn't come padding around the post office corner with a bag in his hands and push his way through the people. The doctor came to the convent twice a year and looked over all the kids in case we were diseased. He was a decent old stick, even though he had bad breath. As soon as I saw him I realized that it had been the Hindu fruiterer behind the window I smashed; now that I thought of it, the face I had seen was pretty much like the Hindu's, although why I didn't recognize him at the time I couldn't say.

That's when I made another discovery about myself—that I wasn't really frightened. I knew the Hindu couldn't say much more than the names of fruit and vegetables and how much they cost, that it would take him about a week to explain exactly what had happened to him, provided he knew himself. And I remember Mum saying that everybody was complaining that he charged too much. And there was a time when the policeman had been to see him about something he had said to Mrs Carroll. A bunch of us kids had made a special trip into town at the lunch hour about six months before to have a look at him when we heard about that. Joseph Kane was scared, so we had only looked into the shop from the other side of the street. We never

114

knew what he had actually said to Mrs Carroll. Legs Hope said it was probably something to do with her being a Presbyterian.

So I knew there wouldn't be anybody who would fuss much about the Hindu. So I wasn't frightened. In fact, I began to feel tougher. I took another stone out of my pocket and started bashing it against the bottom of the memorial, against the words 'In memory of those brave men of Raggleton who laid down their lives for King and country in the Great War, 1914-18.' Underneath, there was a new set of words, not chiselled in the stone like the others, but on a bronze plate, saying, 'In proud memory of the men of this town who died while serving their country, 1939-45.' I thought of all those dead men, of how tough they must have been, and of how many Germans and Japanese they must have killed before they copped it themselves, and how, when they were my age, they had probably been too scared to smash a shop window in somebody's face, although they might have been tough with some old lady. I chipped away with my stone, thinking of a thumping great memorial for me they might one day build at the other end of town. I'd be standing with my fists clenched and my feet on a pile of broken-up enemies, and there'd be a sign underneath, 'To James Sullivan, v.c., who saved his country in its hour of need.'

I got tired of that nonsense, of course, and took off down to the wharf, hoping to see Bloody Jack. Past the park and along the metal road, across the railway line that went to the freezing works. I bowled along, now and then lashing out in the air with my fists, dying to have a crack at somebody.

The wind was blowing from the direction of the works, and there was a horrible stink in the air. A couple of lighters that took cargo out to the ships across the bar were tied up at the wharf, and some empty railway wagons were standing alongside them. Between two of the wagons and up past the furtherest lighter, I saw Jack sitting on the edge, holding a line in one hand. Beside him was the dirty old sugar sack

115

in which he carted his bait and any fish he caught. He was wrapped up in his dirty old coat, staring into the water, chewing away on his cud like a dirty old monkey. I took a fairly big stone out of my pocket and aimed it carefully at him. As soon as I had thrown it, though, I dropped flat on the ground beside the wheels of a wagon where I couldn't be seen. I knew it was going to hit him, and, sure enough, he let out a noise like a bad cough.

When I heard that, I couldn't stop myself any longer. I got up to my feet, shoved both my hands into my pockets, dragged out two fistfuls of stones, and ran out from behind the wagon. I dropped the stones to the ground, holding back one in each hand.

There was Bloody Jack half crouched up on his feet holding one hand to the side of his face. He was still coughing and moaning and as I watched him the blood started to come through his fingers. He banged his feet up and down as though he was trying to march, and all the time his fishing line, which he had let go, was unwinding in jerky jumps and running out over the edge of the wharf until it gave one big jump and went right over the side. Then he stopped his coughing and started to swear. As he did he looked up and saw me.

'I did it, you old bastard,' I shouted.

Well, you should have seen his face. It was the first time in years, I bet, that he really opened his eyes wide open; usually they only peeped out from under floppy yellow eyelids. He kept holding the side of his bleeding face as though he was having a bad dream, his black fuzzy chin working up and down, and his mouth opening and shutting like a fish when it has been pulled out of water.

'I'm going to bash you to pieces,' I shouted again, and belted another stone at him. He was about ten yards away, and it hit his shoulder. He dropped his hand from his cheek, straightened up, keeping on staring at me as though I was a freak, while the blood dribbled down over his jaw and down his neck.

116

'Jimmy,' he said in a soppy voice, 'what's wrong?'

'I hate you and I'm going to kill you,' I yelled at him.

I shifted the other stone into my throwing hand and flung it at him with all my might. It missed his head by a whisker. Those old eyes of his blew up like skyrockets, and he started walking toward me slowly, one hand held right out in front of him, as though he was in the middle of a fire. Somehow this was what I wanted to happen. I was holding my ground under attack from all my enemies, lashing out at them until they killed me, not giving a damn. I grabbed some more stones out of my pockets and started to throw them at him as hard as I could, screaming at the top of my voice with my eyes closed. If I hit him, and how many times, I don't know. My right arm seemed to be throwing again and again, and it was flashing about in my mind that I must have flattened him when I felt a terrific bash on my ear and another on the elbow of my throwing arm. My shoulder simply went bang and it didn't seem as though I even had an arm any longer. I opened my eyes, still screaming, and saw Jack, bigger than I had ever seen him, standing over me. Sticky red and black and dirty in the face, his eyes wild, his arm raised high. Then there was just his hand slapping down and across me, first on one side of my head and then on the other, and a grip on my shoulder that felt as though it was eating me away. I kept screaming until there was nothing left, and then I closed my eyes, and the next thing, I was flopped on the wharf, not caring, and hearing Jack spluttering and panting a long way away. My head was in my arms and my face against the timber of the wharf. I wouldn't say he had knocked me out, but he must have come pretty darn close to it.

I was still hazy when Jack's arm went under my chest to lever me over on to my back. He was on his knees beside me, and looking down as mad as a meat axe.

'If you try to run away, Jimmy, I'll thrash you to within an inch of your life,' he said, and got to his feet and walked away. I sat up and watched as he went away. I sat up and watched as he went way down to the wharfies' shed, where there was a tap, and splashed his face and head with water. My shoulder was aching and the sides of my face were numb, and one ear felt as though it had been pushed into my head.

He bent over as he dried his face with the inside of the bottom of his coat, and came back. I couldn't help noticing that he really wasn't so old as I had thought. He was doing everything in a hurry, not shuffling about like he used to. He had straightened up a little bit taller than he had been', his eyes were still wide open and bright, and when he spoke he sounded as though he meant business, though he was puffing a bit.

'Now what in the blazes got into you, boy?' he said. 'If you tell me any lies I'll skin the hide off you and even your parents won't recognise you, no sir. A boy like you. My God, I don't believe it. I don't indeed.'

Where the stone had hit him in the cheek was a raw mess with a big hunk of skin missing; as I looked up to him my throat choked up, seeing more drops of blood squeezing up in big dots like that on his face. All I could do was to shake my head.

'I'm going to take you home with me and show your mother and father what you've done. How would you like that, eh?' When I still couldn't say anything, he smacked his hands together and yelled, 'Are you hurt, boy? Stand up and let's see how you are. Stand up now, this minute.'

I pushed myself to my feet and he grabbed me by the shoulders and half squatted so that he could look me level in the face. 'How's your head? You're not dizzy now?' he said. He took my chin and turned my face to each side roughly. Then he grabbed my right arm and said, 'How's the throwing apparatus, eh?' and lifted it up and worked it around and then pushed it up and down from the elbow. 'All honky-dory, boy. Everything still working. Nothing broken.' I nodded my head as he pushed me right away from him and repeated, 'Now, what got into you, boy?'

I suppose I could have talked by now, but I decided it

was no use. I did try to think of an answer to his question, but none came. What I had done was so bad that I couldn't really believe it had anything to do with the actual me. Anyway, I just shook my head again, and after a few minutes of trying to make me talk, Jack got fed up. 'If it wasn't for the fact that all the starch has been knocked out of you, son, and you've always been such a friendly little cuss like, I would see that you got another good whipping from your father, and maybe tell them Roman sisters that teach you what you've done,' he said. 'An old man doesn't much care, and all I'll say is that I never want to see you again down here or near me anywhere.'

He took me by the shoulder, turned me around, and pushed me so hard in the middle of the back that I almost fell over. 'Get along with you, Jimmy,' he said. 'If I ever hear of you throwing stones at anyone else, too, I'll tell the police what you done this afternoon. I'll give you another licking, too. But don't you ever come down to the wharf again, not ever.'

I didn't start walking straight away. He gave me a push in the seat of my pants with his foot, as though I was a mongrel dog hanging around trying to steal his bait. I moved away slowly, not hardly feeling or thinking, just going, dumb as though I was loony, off the wharf, across the railway line, up to the park, where I crawled under some bushes for a while and cried a bit.

That was the last time I went on the wharf.

16

MOLLY wasn't at home then, of course, and I can't help hating her for not being there. She was a girl, and nearly seventeen, while I was only eleven, and a boy. She might have made all the difference to me, and even to Mum and Dad. But while all this was happening she was hundreds of miles away in Wellington, having a good old time in the convent down there, with not a care. If she had been home, nothing might have happened. But she hadn't been home for nearly three months, since Easter. I don't suppose I should blame her, because she didn't ask to be sent away to the convent, and it was a fact that there was no secondary school she could have gone to in our town. Raggleton wasn't that big. And yet it was so wrong for me to be up to my neck in trouble like that, and her not at all.

Molly only came home for holidays, which were pretty short, except at Christmas, when she had six weeks off. Even then, she spent only half the time at home, the rest of the time going off to stay in the country with that tall skinny girl, Maggie Robinson. She hardly even bothered to take any notice of me that last Christmas, either. I mean, if she had any sense at all she might have at least sat down and had a good talk with me, and passed on some knowledge of the outside world or something like that. Not that I mind her not doing it, really.

But if she had been around when Bloody Jack had booted me off the wharf that time, I might have gone and told her about it. I might even have talked to her about Mum and Dad fighting on top of the steps, and Mum falling, and my thinking about it so hard afterward that I kidded myself into seeing God hanging around. Heck, you're practically grown up when you are nearly seventeen and should be able to explain what goes on.

And I might as well admit that I felt there might be some hope for Molly when last she came home. After she went off to that Maggie's place after Christmas I was very annoyed with her, but when she came home at Easter I couldn't help being impressed by the way she was growing up. She was getting to be good-looking, and really like a woman.

Mum and I met her when she got off the railway bus at the post office. The stop was a few yards around the corner from the main street, and we waited under the verandah of the bookshop next to the post office, as it was raining slightly. The post office was a two-story brick building that looked like a castle, yet it had no verandah. All the other shops and buildings had these verandahs that came right out over the footpath, so it didn't matter a darn whether it rained or not; you never got wet. The post office was the best building in Raggleton except for that.

Well, the bus pulled up, and the people climbed out looking very creased and tired, and Molly was the last person off. You could have knocked me down with a feather when I laid eyes on her. She was wearing a pink dress that had no neck—that is, it didn't start until it was a good way down her chest—and carrying her coat over her arm. She and Mum kissed each other and then she bent down and gave me a peck. I was all set to give her some cheek, but I forgot all about that. Then this bloke who was another passenger came up and smiled all over his face, and said, 'Can I get your bags off, Miss Sullivan?' and she gave him a smile, and answered in a la-di-da voice, 'Oh, that would be so kind of you,' and he rushed to the back of the bus and hauled out her two bags and rushed them over as though he was being paid for the job.

'Thank you very much,' Molly said. 'My brother will carry the smaller one, and I'll leave the other for Father to pick up later.'

'Thank you, young man,' Mum said, not looking nearly as

friendly as Molly, and he shuffled and grinned, and said, 'I'll see you about, then.' Molly came up with an even bigger smile as he walked away and said, 'Thanks, loads,' and held up one hand and waved her fingers as though she was Lady Muck.

'Well, I must say.' Mum sounded huffy.

'Don't be silly, Mother. He was a nice boy and we talked on the way up. What on earth is the matter with that?'

'The dress you are wearing.' Mum sounded huffier than ever.

'Oh, dear, Mother, it was so terribly warm in Wellington, and you can't imagine the relief it is to get out of school uniform into something decent.' Molly's voice was different, too—it had a lot of side, and went up and down like the scales on a piano. 'I made it myself in sewing class, although Sister Monica would have had a blue fit if she had bothered to have a look at the pattern.'

I looked hard at her, still surprised: she always had a nice face. Now it was absolutely terrific, with her big blue eyes, red lips, and pink-and-yellow skin and crinkly hair; even her arms and legs looked grown up. All this must have been going on for a long time, of course: seeing her dressed like that after just a few months made it hit me all of a sudden.

'Bless my heart and soul, you've got lipstick on, too,' Mum said.

Molly giggled and said, 'Oh, Mother, you are sounding terribly old-fashioned, y'know.'

I didn't even talk to her until after we had arrived home, beyond answering her hoity-toity questions, like, 'Are you working hard at school, Jimmy?' And actually, Mum and her didn't talk much, either. As we walked, with Molly carrying her own bag, incidentally—that stuff about me carrying it was so much bullo when she was talking to that bloke—there were only odd bits of chit-chat with long silences between.

As we were on the last stretch of road leading to home, Molly looked so seriously around her, at the lupines and marram grass, and scuffed the stones of the footpath with her shoes, and then stared at our house.

'I do wish the old place could be painted, Mum,' she said. That was the first time she had used the word, 'Mum,' so I suppose she was beginning to feel more like she was in the old days.

Another thing she said was, 'How's Dad?' Mum answered, 'Your father is all right,' and that was all Molly knew about the whole business.

It had stopped raining by this time, but everything was dripping; there were small puddles in the road and even the air seemed heavy and wet; as we got to the gate water was leaking from the spouting of the roof and running down the side of the house in a tiny stream. It was definitely the end of the summer.

'I would like to go for a swim,' Molly said. 'Would you come with me, Jimmy? I feel so sticky after all that time in a bus.'

'We'll see,' I said, not wanting to let on that I thought it was not quite the weather for swimming. It certainly was still warm, and only four o'clock in the afternoon but I never did see the sense in swimming in the rain or any time except when you are feeling hot.

But she insisted, once we got inside. She became more like the Molly of years before, rushing around in a great frit, digging up some old bathing costume because she had left her other one behind in Wellington, and laughing at Mum when she said, 'Really, Molly, you've hardly set foot in the house when you're up to silliness again.'

So we set off, with our costumes wrapped in towels, and I couldn't help feeling pleased, even though I didn't much want to swim. It was the first time in a year that Molly had even bothered to do anything with me.

We took the short cut to the beach, from behind our place, through the marram grass, around the borough rubbish tip, over the sand hills, and through the lupines that ended at the edge of the beach.

123

'I had to get away, and I really wanted a swim,' Molly told me. 'I always think of the fun I used to have swimming, and I could see Mum was getting into a bad mood, so I thought, Well, old girl, you had better take a swim now, and it will be no lecture for you.'

'Mum wasn't in a bad mood,' I said. 'She was only quiet —she gets like that now and then.'

'I've only come home because I had to,' Molly said. 'There was nothing else for me to do, and the sisters would have thought it strange if I had stayed on at the convent during Easter.'

'It would be very funny, that's why,' I explained. 'What's wrong with coming home, anyway?'

Molly looked at me, her big eyes drippy, and patted me on the head. 'You wouldn't understand, Jimmy. You're not old enough. There are better places than Raggleton though, and there are better places than home.'

'Golly, it's all right for you to say that, but you've got to have a home, and next year you will have finished school and have to come back home all the time. Dad says he can get you a job in the harbour board office.'

'I'll have something to say about that when the time comes,' she said. 'You like it at home, do you?'

'That's silly, Molly,' I told her. 'Home's home. You can't get away from that can you? Home is home and that's where you live and that's all there is to it.'

'I'm glad for you, Jimmy,' she said. 'I suppose it must be a whole lot better for you, being so young. You are lucky.'

I was getting less pleased with her. All I said was 'You're getting your new dress wet,' as we came out through the lupines and on to the beach.

'It's not a new dress, and I don't care,' she said. 'Is the hide-out still there or do we have to go way down to the dressing sheds?'

The hide-out was a clearing back in the lupines not far along the beach: it was against a cliff face, and we kids used to use it as a base whenever we were down about there. It

124

gave me a big kick to see Molly didn't think she was too grown up to go there.

'Of course,' I said, and led the way down a side track. The wet lupines brushed against us, showering our bodies with drops of rain, and Molly's pink dress was dreadfully blotched and sticking to her when we finally got out into the clearing, yet she didn't give a darn. We turned our backs on each other as we always had done, undressed and put our togs on; at least I got my togs on, and Molly nearly did.

'Isn't this maddening?' she said. 'You'll have to help me, Jimmy.'

I killed myself laughing at her when I turned around, and I'll say this much for her, she laughed too. Her costume used to be one of those that come up the front and tied around the back of the neck; now it came some of the way up and over the front, and the straps could no longer reach around her neck. Anyway, I fished out a piece of string from the pocket of my pants, and between the two of us we joined the short ends behind her neck, and that kept everything up, although, as she said, the string was uncomfortable and cut into her skin. Then I had to scout up and down our part of the beach to see that nobody else was around before she would come out of the lupines and have a swim.

'It would be utterly humiliating to be seen like this,' Molly explained.

Nobody did see her and we had a short swim. The water was cold and we were both glad to run back to the hide-out. I had my pants and shirt on before she had even finished drying her hair, and then, darn me, she couldn't get the the string around her neck undone because the knot had been pulled so tight and was wet. We each tried separately to snap the string. We couldn't, so we both tried together. She held the string over one shoulder with both hands and leaned down so that I could pull from the other side. I gave an almighty heave, the string snapped and she straightened up at the same time. There was a ripping sound and I had torn everything off right down to her belly button.

Well, it was funny as the dickens, her standing there with her mouth open and her eyes bulging.

I doubled up laughing, I mean I couldn't help looking at her, as it was by far the most wind that I had ever seen taken out of her sails.

'Give me my towel, Jimmy,' she yelled.

'Golly,' I said, 'I must say you've got as grown up as they come,' and then I went right on laughing. She spluttered and frowned and said a few 'oh, ohs' in an excited voice, and unwound her arms and bent down and picked up the towel herself.

It was beginning to hurt to laugh so much, but as I stopped she gave an awful giggle, and that set me off again until my stomach really ached.

'It's just as well you are my brother, that's all I can say,' Molly said, looking like a white native, if you know what I mean. Her hair was all frizzed up where she had dried it with the towel, and she had practically nothing on. She had come on, there was no doubt about that, and I couldn't help being impressed because she had looked very fit standing there with her good-looking face as bright as a button, her skin a white-gold kind of a mixture, and her thingumabobs standing out like nobody's business with bits of orange peel on top.

'Turn around, the joke's over,' she said.

'Was that utterly humiliating?' I said, doing as she told me without arguing, because, really, she had been pretty decent not to get wild.

'Utterly and completely,' she said.

'Well, you certainly have got a whopping chest,' I said.

'How dare you say that, Jimmy. It is not whopping, I'll have you know. These togs must be three years old if they're a day, and I'm much bigger now. That's natural.'

'I'll say you are.'

'If you must know, I've got the best measurements a girl could have. You'll get bigger, too, y'know, when you grow up.'

'If I want a big chest I have to go in for weight-lifting and deep breathing and physical jerks and all that, really working for it like, but with you, yours just grew without any trouble, as far as I can see.'

She tittered away and said, 'You've seen far more than you should have, not that it matters when you're my little brother. Y'know, Jimmy, I'm glad you are my little brother. You say the funniest things.'

'Do I? Well you looked pretty funny.'

I turned around as she finished hauling her dress down over her head. She smoothed it down over herself, patting it here and there, and then took a deep breath and pressed her hands hard against her waist and stood up on her bare toes in the sand, as though she was a dancer.

'My, don't we like ourselves,' I kidded her.

She let out her breath, and flopped back on her heels. She looked full of beans and mischief and excitement.

'You don't know how lucky I am, Jimmy,' she said. 'I'm the right height, and I've got a flat tummy and a good bust, a high one, too, and that's important, and good legs, and I've always been pretty. I'm so lucky because I'm going to get a rich husband and he'll take me a million miles away, and I'll never, never come back here.'

'What about me?' I said.

'I'll send for you. You can come and live with us if you want to.'

'What if I don't want to come?' I said. 'And you are talking very early, aren't you? You haven't stopped growing. Your tummy might get fat and your chest might get too big. It seems pretty darn big to me already.'

She flicked her wet towel around my legs and said, 'You're impossible, Jimmy. A naughty, impossible little boy. I don't know why I bother with you.'

Molly was home for four days—it was the last time she ever came home—and I couldn't help noticing that she wasn't the slightest bit interested in Mum and Dad. When she spoke to them she always sounded snooty. I don't think

127

Dad minded, because I heard him telling her, 'You're a real lady, aren't you, Molly? You've got connections on your father's side, and all the Sullivan women have been ladies. It is a matter of breeding.' It was Mum who was annoyed, and she and Molly had some kind of argument the second day Molly was home; I don't know what it was about, but Molly walked out of the house, slamming doors behind her, and didn't come back till late in the afternoon. I think she must have gone to the pictures, because this was a Saturday.

But she never heard Mum and Dad fighting, and she never saw Dad drunk. Yet she thought she was having a bad time. Once I went into her bedroom and found her lying on the floor with a pillow under her head, looking at the ceiling like death warmed up. Even though I never let her know, I saw that Molly was beautiful. She was built like these women on the covers of magazines, the ones who are always stretched out backward over rocks, or sitting on some sultan's sofa dressed in beads, and she had a face like the Virgin Mary's in religious paintings. Flopped out on the floor like that she looked so terribly sad that I tried to cheer her up by offering to play a game of cards with her.

'No thanks, Jimmy,' she whispered, rolling her blue eyes so far sideways away from me that they turned white.

'What's wrong?' I said.

'Nothing,' she said.

That's why I feel annoyed with Molly; she missed everything, and yet when she was home she behaved as though she was the unluckiest person in the whole world. Except for when we were down at the beach, she was either snooty or sad. And the time I really could have done with some help from her was after Bloody Jack had kicked me off the wharf.

After I crawled out from under the bushes in the park, and went around the side streets back through town, in case they were still fussing over the Hindu fruiterer, I went back to school and picked up my new bike. I was so tired and worn-out that it was a great effort to get my legs to pedal the darn thing. My head was throbbing, too.

If only Molly had been around then. It was all very well to have a flat tummy and a good bust and legs, as she said, and it might help a girl to have them, and yet it would have been better of her to be around at the right time. Then I wouldn't have cared if she was the ugliest girl in the world.

17

'You like the bike I gave you?' That was the first thing Dad said to me when he saw me. He was sitting on a chair in the kitchen as though he was about to fall off it; his face was so red, and it looked as though it had leaked over into his eyes.

I had been laying on my bed since I had got home because I wasn't feeling well, and didn't want to be seen. Mum thought I was reading, and didn't bother me till tea was ready at about seven o'clock; that's when I went along to the kitchen.

Because I know now what was about to happen to him, I feel sorry for Dad. If he really did come from such a high and mighty family, if he really did own a lot of race horses when he was young and was a great friend of famous people, he must have been sorry for himself, too. The depression really was to blame, I suppose. Dad always spoke of the depression as though it was a horrible disease that had nearly killed him; everything that had happened to him, he once told me, was caused by the depression and Mum.

The depression must have been worse than war, because he always seemed pleased with himself when he talked about the First World War, in spite of the fact that once he told me that it was in some hand-to-hand fighting there that his arm had been mangled. Even during the last war, when I was only a kid, I can remember him getting excited and talking about it as though it was a wonderful thing. And after that war was over he was all for getting stuck into Russia.

'The filthy Communists should be wiped off the map,' he said. 'We've cleaned up Hitler so we might as well wipe the floor with Stalin while we are at it. I wouldn't mind getting into that fight myself if I wasn't too old.'

Yet now and then he would talk about the depression, and he would be very different.

'I hope you never have to live through another depression, Jimmy,' he would say. 'It ruined your father.'

So you see, when I say that the depression was worse than the war, I know what I'm talking about, even if I'm not sure of the exact details.

I will always see Dad as he was sitting in that chair in the kitchen, with his black shoes unlaced and with the tongues pulled up so that they would be more comfortable, his legs sagging out at the knees pulling his trousers way up over his socks, showing his hairy calves, the top of his trousers unbuttoned and his braces unhitched, his waistcoat open, his collar and tie off, his right arm holding over the back of the chair allowing him to hang forward: if it hadn't been for that arm holding him I'm darned sure he would have flopped right over. The breath was coming out of his mouth and nose as though he was blowing and sucking, and his face, besides being so darn red, was puffed and sweating. Boy, he was drunk. I had got so that I could smell beer on Dad a mile off; I could have smelled it then from a hundred miles away.

Yet he spoke quite clearly, which still puzzles me. Usually he got his words mixed up and slurred; yet this time, though he was the worst I had ever seen him, he sounded as clear as a bell.

'You like that bike I gave you?' he said.

I was stiff and sore. That business in the afternoon and the bashing from Bloody Jack had taken all the stuffing out of me. Yet it had made me nearly forget about the trouble of the morning. Now my forgetting was all over, and I started to feel cold. I looked at Mum as she was dishing out a stew from a pot on the stove, although I didn't need to look to know how she was feeling.

'I've forgotten to wash my hands,' I said, turning back and going out of the kitchen. I was afraid that I would have one of my queer turns in front of them. I don't suppose there was any danger, really, but I went to the bathroom and washed myself with hot water, said a Hail Mary, and sang 'It's a Long Way to Tipperary' as I dried myself, as a precaution.

Dad heard me singing, because he started up on the same song himself, and kept it up until I got back.

'That's a great old song you're trying to sing, Jimmy, and I'm glad you are so happy to sing a great old song like that. Why are you singing, eh?'

Mum put the plates on the table as he was talking, gave a hiss like a railway engine blowing off steam, and then glared at him. She didn't say a word. That did it for me. Suddenly everything inside me, inside my head and my body, just lay down. It was as though what was me had been held up by a piece of string which had snapped and let me fall. It was a wonderful feeling, honestly; a little like the way you get when you are in a hot bath too long. I couldn't even care or worry if I tried; if a pin had been stuck into me, I probably wouldn't have felt it.

'I was singing because I was singing, I suppose,' I said to Dad.

He sat up in his chair and pulled it over to his place at the table. 'You are happy, Jimmy, old boy, old boy. That's why you sing, because you are happy. Your old Dad has made you happy with that bike, and don't you worry, your old Dad is going to do lots of things for you, old son, old son. He's going to see you get the chance he didn't have, and he's going to see you don't get the rotten luck he had. You can't keep a Sullivan down, because they didn't really lick your old man, no sir. They just gave him rotten luck and smashed him up and tied him to a she-devil. They didn't lick him, by God no. They held him down and they'll have to keep holding me down, but he'll not give in, no sir. They'll have to hold him down till the day he dies. And by God I bet they do hold him down, not giving him a chance.'

I shovelled my stew down, not bothering to look up. I was on one side of the table, Mum was on the other side, and Dad sat at the top talking his head off. As though it was somebody else, and nothing to do with me, I felt Mum getting boiling mad. I felt it, yet I didn't care. Except for the time she was at the stove, I hadn't even looked at her, and I wasn't going to either.

'Sure I take a few drinks, son,' Dad said. 'I take a few drinks and I can hold my drinks, as I've been around and no gentleman ever gets so drunk he can't control himself, so you never have to be ashamed of me, not in your sweet life you don't. You don't have to be ashamed of me. Don't I see that you get what you need, and a good bike that is, too, as good as any boy your age in this town or anywhere in the country? By God I can still see that my son gets a fair deal. They can't stop me from doing that, no, sir, and I'll see that you don't get tied up with the wrong kind of woman if it is the last thing I do. There are lots of ignorant slobs of women waiting to get their clutches on you and when they do they turn their filthy backs on you and what you do is give them a boot in their backsides if you are a man, and you will be a man because you are a Sullivan.'

I kept scooping the food into my mouth, staring hard at the stuff as it came up to my mouth on the fork, and when Mum whispered, 'If you don't stop that I'll kill you,' I wasn't even surprised; it was as though I had heard her say it before she actually spoke.

Dad's voice was still as clear as a bell, except that it seemed to have faded, and he said, 'I'm talking to my son, woman, so you keep your mouth shut.'

Mum said something else that I didn't quite hear; then Dad whispered again from a long way away. I tried to jiggle my brain along so that I could hear them, but the effort was too much. I was tired out, and instead of not being able to keep my eyes open, the way it usually is when you are that far gone, I couldn't keep my ears listening. Their voices were there, yet they sounded so light that as soon as they reached me they were gone before I could actually hear the words. A sort of happiness filled me up, the way it does when you

133

are three-quarters asleep, warm in bed, and drifting around all over the place as though you are floating. All I could see, too, was my plate, and my knife and fork in my hands, silently moving. I dropped my knife without a sound and shifted the fork over to my right hand and scooped the last of the stew into my mouth. I could see the thin crack on the plate, and I stared at it till it wriggled. I took a deep breath and looked up, and I think I said, 'I'm tired now and I want to go to bed.' That's what I meant to say, and my lips moved and my voice must have sounded, yet the words were swallowed up into thin air.

The skin on Mum's face was somehow stretched so tight that it looked as though the bones underneath were going to burst out; her shoulders were hunched up, her eyes were shining, her nose was white and her lips yellow, and there were black-stretched lines on her neck. I didn't care. Dad was ticking his head from side to side and all the red in his face and eyes was bright as new paint and he had this smile with his lips pulled back and set, as though they were always like that, never shifting, and somehow I could see that he was in some kind of happiness, too; he looked as though he was doing what he had always wanted to do. All I could do was see, and that is what I saw; Dad glowing as if he was heading for the winning post a hundred yards ahead of anybody else, and it was something to do with my mother wound up so tight and hard that all her skin was stretched. I didn't care how they looked, though, and after I had said what I thought I said, and both their lips moved, I got around from behind the table and went to the door and closed it behind me.

The lock clicked so loudly and my ears jumped in an awful ache that was gone before I could even feel it, and all the faraway things rushed in close to me again. From the other side of the door I heard him say, 'I've got you, and when I've finished with you it'll be back into the gutter.' The air moved in closer to me, too, and became colder and colder as my heart began to thump harder and harder. I

134

turned down toward the bathroom and ran to turn the tap on before I exploded. I was careful not to sing too loudly this time.

That night I had the only dream I ever remembered completely afterwards. I must have gone to sleep as soon as I was in bed, because I remember nothing until I walked into this huge spider web that stretched from the earth to the sky. At first I enjoyed myself, pulling at the strands that were as thick as ropes, and watching the whole web shiver and shake for as far as I could see, miles and miles up and around myself. But when I tried to go away the web stuck to my hands and legs, and the ropes shrivelled up until they were thin and cold. Then I was slowly lifted up until my feet were off the ground and my arms were stretched wide out. There was a tugging at my wrists. I tried to struggle and kick my way out but it was no use. I let myself hang and waited.

The whole web bounced as though some huge creature had landed on the outer edge on a lot of different legs. The strands that held me started to hum like telegraph wires in a high wind and slowly I could feel this big thing feel its way toward me. I tore at my arms and legs to try and get free. 'Let me go, let me go,' I screamed at the top of my voice, and the web began to jump up and down like crazy as this thing got nearer. 'Let me go, please,' I yelled again, and then started saying 'please, please,' over and over again.

A light flashed in my eyes and a voice called to me, 'Jimmy, it's all right,' and the light flashed off and on, each time stronger, until my eyes were wide open to it, and stinging, and slowly seeing a figure, a big figure, coming into shape.

'You've had a bad dream, son, that's all,' the voice said.

It was Mum. She was standing at the foot of the bed. It was such a huge relief seeing her there.

'You've overtired yourself on that bike,' she said, 'and you've had a bad dream that is all over now. It's all over now.'

'I'm sorry,' I said.

'Back to sleep, boy. And what have you got your arms stretched out like that for, silly? Tuck them back under the blankets.'

I turned over on my side and pulled my arms against my chest and felt her hands pull the blankets over my shoulders tightly and shove the ends hard under the mattress; so hard that I was pushed up and dropped down again.

I meant to ask her what time it was but all I could raise was a mumble and I didn't feel like trying again. And then it came to me that she had her clothes on; I was going to ask her why she was dressed, but when I opened my eyes again the light had been turned off and she had gone. And when I woke up in the morning her being dressed was the first thought I had; it was strange because for all I knew it might have been very early in the night when she had come into my bedroom, and as she wouldn't have gone to bed then it was natural that she would still have her clothes on. Yet I was worried. I kicked back my blankets and went over the whole business, even the bad dream I'd had, and thought of the blurred way Mum looked at me after I had half wakened up. It came to me in one big bang, of course; she had different clothes on from what she had been wearing at tea-time the night before. I stopped worrying about it all then.

18

I WAS still feeling dead when I got up, and all during break-fast I was so dopey that I didn't catch on at first. My head felt too heavy as I messed around with my porridge. Mum hadn't said a word to me—I hadn't even seen her, except for her back. She stood at the sink polishing the silver: it was a queer time to be doing that, I thought, and tried to wake myself up properly by pinching my cheeks with my left hand. My eyelids felt as though they were made of sticky paper, and it seemed that there was nothing inside me except the hot feeling of the porridge: no blood, bones, or guts or anything like that. Funny, though, it was not exactly a bad way to be, and I decided to make the most of it while it lasted: I looked at the walls, and saw how different they were, with all their marks and streaks alive and shifting, the electric light bulb hanging down from the ceiling like a big round white eye, the stove hot and bulging, the linoleum on the floor sighing up and down with some strange wind blowing underneath, the cupboard doors half opened, letting cups and plates stare out at me from the darkness behind. But I wasn't frightened. If the whole house was going to start mucking itself around, that was all right by me.

Then I got interested, and actually stared at Mum's back to see if she was different, too. I stared at her tweed costume skirt and blouse, half expecting them to play some tricks in front of my eyes. For a second there it looked as though those dots like sand in the tweed were going to run around all over the place, and I wondered if the clothes would shift off her back altogether, and leave her standing in her shimmy. But it was me and the house that changed. Without actually looking I could feel the whole place becoming the same as it was the day before, and every yesterday there'd ever been, and that's what happened to me, too. All my blood and guts came back and my old brain clicked as I caught on that the skirt and blouse were the same as Mum had worn when she came to me after my bad dream. They were her Sunday clothes, as a matter of fact.

The dopey feeling was running away from me, even though I didn't want it to; I didn't mind feeling as dead as a doornail. But in a minute I became alive and excited. And listening. I was listening with my head cocked on one side, and I didn't even know what I was listening for until I couldn't hear it, if you know what I mean. There were no sounds at all, and that was why I was listening. Except for the clink, clink of Mum dropping the silver into their places, the whole house was silent.

'Where's Dad?' I asked.

If he had been around, or running late for breakfast, I would have heard him thumping and bumping around upstairs, and knocking around in the bathroom; anything like that I would have heard. But I couldn't hear any movement whatever. He wasn't around; and Mum, she was dressed up in her best clothes.

Mum straightened right up at the sink and stood there as though she was at attention.

'He got up early and left, son,' she said. Her voice was different.

'What for? He has never done that before.'

'Business, that's all. Finish your porridge; hurry up.'

Instead of my stopping to think, or being thrown off by the sound of her voice, I felt even more excited.

'What business? He couldn't have any business like that, could he?'

Her hand flew right out from her side and then slapped hard down on the sink bench, and she said, 'Don't pester me, Jimmy, and finish up your breakfast and get off to school.'

She looked over her shoulder at me as she spoke and it hit me the same way as when I had a shock off the cord of

138

our electric iron. All the lines of her face had become jumbled up and they were this way here and that way there, her cheeks sagged like an old woman's, and her eyes were pushed back right into her head.

All my life my mother had nearly always looked at me as though she liked me tremendously—that is, except when she was mad at me over some little thing I might have done wrong, or when she was busy, or, as lately, when she looked at me as though she wasn't even thinking of me (I didn't mind that, actually). When she looked at me most of the time, though, I could see that I gave her a big kick. But the look she gave me now was so different that I stared right into her queer eyes, I was so surprised, and she turned away from me quickly.

For some reason, I started to think of a dog that was run over outside school one playtime. Joe and I were leaning over the fence when it cut right across the road in front of us and was belted by a wool truck. The dog turned right over in mid-air and was tossed back on the footpath right under our noses, landing on its belly, nose flopped up against the fence, head pushed right back, and legs spread-eagled out. That way, all in a sudden bang, and I looked down straight into its eyes; they stared at me for a second as though they saw what happened to every living thing that was ever hurt, and then the light in them turned off. Joe and I both yelled, and the driver came running back and tossed a sack over the dog and put it on the back of the truck. He was pretty upset himself, though he did his best not to let on. He said the dog was killed straight away, and never felt any pain. I knew better.

And now, after a year or more, I thought of the way that dog looked at me. Then I reminded myself that it was the look Mum gave me that was really worrying me, and I tried to separate the two and couldn't. I knew then it was going to be another rotten day for me.

While I was staring at her, Mum reached out across her body with her right arm to pick up a duster at the end of

139

the sink. A long red scratch ran all the way from her wrist up the inside of her arm until it disappeared under the sleeve of her blouse. It looked like a long red worm.

I shut my eyes hard, because I was getting so darn boiled up that I was almost sick. When I opened my eyes again she had pulled her arm back. The trouble was, I didn't feel dull and dopey; instead, I was so keyed up I felt like screaming all over the house, or taking off in a run and not stopping until I was halfway around the world.

I told myself it was all because I hadn't had enough sleep. And she hadn't had enough sleep, either, what with my waking up in the middle of the night with my bad dreams. And with Dad getting up early and going away—he must have done that, because she said so—it meant she had to get up early. So with the two of us, she just hadn't got enough sleep. That was it. Not enough sleep, and now she was looking a wreck. Like that big advertisement for cocoa, with the woman snuggled up under a ton of blankets with her hand tucked underneath her chin and a little smile on her mouth and the sign underneath saying something about a wise woman who drinks this stuff will get plenty of sleep and stay beautiful. Another picture showed some old hag glaring out from under the same blankets on the same bed and the sign saying that her sleepless night would ruin her looks because she didn't drink this stuff. I thought of myself in an advertisement picture, a wild look in my eyes, knocking the hell out of the Hindu fruiterer and the sign asking parents if they wanted their children to behave like this. Boy, what an advertisement I would have made for cocoa.

I cleaned up the rest of my porridge and said at the top of my voice, to show her that I didn't feel any different from usual, 'I've finished, Mum, so I'll get cracking.'

She didn't answer, so I headed on out, and as soon as I was in the passage I felt cold patches of air blowing around. That was queer, because whenever I was alone in the house with either Mum or Dad, there was never any suggestion of my feeling like that, and the house was never unfriendly.

140

Yet now my skin thickened up a little, and my heart gave a couple of thumps, and the marble feeling was near as I looked up the stairs to my parents' room. I dived along the passage to my own room, grabbed my schoolbag and tore out again, shoved my head in the kitchen door and shouted, 'See you tonight, Mum,' and tore across the porch to the back door.

As soon as I hit the fresh air, I took a couple of deep breaths and felt better. It was one of those mornings that tasted like a really good apple. The old sea was booming softly away over there at the back, the cold was steaming up to the sun, which was just getting properly under way, and you got the impression that anything that went wrong in the whole darned world the day before was going to get another chance. I went and took my bike up from the side of the house and pushed it up to the path through the gate, listening to the scratching noise the tyres made as they bit into the gravel, when I heard Mum call out, 'Wait for me, Jimmy. I'm going to the village. I'll walk with you to the corner.' She was hurrying up the path after me, pulling on her coat, pushing the collar right up around her cheeks. It wasn't cold, either. She didn't wear a hat, which was funny, too. I had never seen her going anywhere without a hat. And she didn't even look at me, only came through the gate and turned on down the road with quick steps, leaving me to push my bike beside her.

'You'll have to slow down a bit, Mum,' I said, feeling a little giddy, and longing to ask her where she was going.

Then there was the way she walked. She used to move very steadily, one long step after another, and now I was listening to her feet going pit-pat, pit-pat, in little short hops, and it wasn't because she was going slow because of me. I had walked beside her plenty of times, sometimes when we were carrying loads of shopping and only just crawling along, and her feet never sounded like that. I stared down at the ground and saw that nothing was wrong with her shoes. She wasn't limping. Her feet were going up and down

141

in jerks, without covering much ground in a stride. I tried to kid myself that that was the way she always walked; it looked different, that's all, because we both needed some sleep.

I felt ashamed because we hadn't spoken to each other. And I tried to think of some question to ask, or some remark to pass that would get her talking. Nothing would come. I closed my eyes tight for a second, took one hand off the handle bars and rubbed my head to stir up my brain. What came up was, 'Mum, is it all right my having the bike?' She didn't answer, so I asked her again.

'Oh, yes, that,' she said.

'Is it all right?'

'Yes,' she said. What she said floated out of her mouth; it was her voice, but it sounded as though she had lent it to somebody else and they were using it, if you know what I mean.

'I didn't really want this bike,' I explained. 'Now that I've got it, I'm glad I have, thought it wouldn't have killed me not to have it, and I wouldn't mind giving it back or anything like that.'

'Give what back?' she said, this time looking down at me, and again I was frightened by her funny eyes.

'The bike.'

'Oh,' she said. 'It's your bike, son. There's nobody to give it back to.' And she looked ahead again.

'Where are you going, Mum?' I popped that one out in a hurry, I was feeling so messed around. She didn't answer, and I didn't mind; she obviously didn't want to talk, so that was that as far as I was concerned. I had done my best.

We reached the corner at last, and I pushed my bike out to the edge of the road, and said, 'Well, see you later, Mum.'

She said, 'I'm sorry, Jimmy. When you grow up, remember I said I was sorry.'

She stood there, holding her green coat about her tightly, so funny and worn-out and old, so completely different from what she had ever been that I couldn't quite feel it was my mother: her face was so white, and all those drooping lines, and her eyes like holes in the ground. I must have looked different to her, too, because somehow or other things were all changed between us. Yet I didn't worry because I knew why I was different and I was sure I would change back again, and she would, too. The way I had behaved the day before, I had to take that into consideration. A kid of my age couldn't do all those things and expect nothing to be changed the next day.

And then, believe it or not, it came to me for the first time that all the difference was caused by me; that poor old woman I had given a bad time, the Hindu whose face was probably cut to pieces, and Bloody Jack, blood streaming down the side of his face, knocked half out of his mind by the stones I threw at him. The police must have found out, and Dad had to go away early to see what could be done; he was probably at the station now. And Mum was one her way down to join him, letting me go on to school until they knew exactly what was to be done with me.

'That's all right, Mum,' I said. 'I'm sorry, too. Don't worry about me.'

'Good-bye, son,' she said, as if I hadn't said anything at all, and then turned and walked towards town.

'I didn't mean anything, Mum. It came over me, that's all,' I called after her.

But she didn't hear me somehow or other, even though I could hear her new kind of walk going pit-pat, pit-pat on the footpath.

I couldn't understand why she didn't ask me why I had done what I had, and somehow let me know that nothing too bad would happen to me. Standing there watching her go, I felt lonelier than I have ever been in my life. You must remember this was more than two years ago, and I was only eleven, and still not tough enough not to care. I decided that the situation must be so bad she couldn't even talk about it yet: perhaps Bloody Jack had died, for he was an old man, and couldn't be expected to take too much rough stuff without kicking the bucket, or the Hindu might have lost his eyes when the glass smashed into him. Whatever it was, it was so bad that she couldn't do anything for me.

19

NOTHING was changed at school. Nobody seemed to know a darned thing about what had happened in town. Even in a big place like Raggleton, the kids most times would know if somebody had smashed a shop window. Not this time, they didn't, though. Joe Waters and the others yarned away while we were waiting for the bell to go before classes, and didn't even notice anything different about me. Golly, they were great friends, Joe and Sniffy, Legs and the rest. They didn't hold it against me that I hadn't played with them the day before; didn't even mention it, in fact. So I could lean against the wall of the school nodding my head and grunting, without actually having to do any talking myself, while they nattered their heads off. They got around to the subject of girls. Sniffy had been reading a book and come across some word in it that I can't remember. Anyway, he had looked it up in some medical book his mother kept at the back of the linen cupboard and there was a whole lot of stuff on the one word, and Sniffy said it was the truth. I didn't pay much attention; I was waiting for the worst to happen. Exactly what was going to happen to me I didn't know, but I knew something was going to hit any minute.

Joe and Legs got into a heck of an argument on whether everybody did what this word said they did when they grew up, Joe saying he wasn't going to, for one, and Legs saying that some woman would make him, otherwise she wouldn't marry him. Joe said he bet kings and queens didn't come at such silly rot, and neither would he, even if it meant he didn't get married. All this stuff never interested me much. Perhaps it was because I had a sister like Molly, and knew she was pretty much the same as anybody else, except for her build, especially the chest part, which looked a handicap, if anything, the last time I had seen it that time on the beach.

The bell ended all that talk, and we went into class and said our prayers. Sister Angela always thought we were better than usual the day after confession, I suppose because none of us had had time to do much sinning. So she always tossed in a couple of extra prayers for us to say out loud, to help keep our slates clean until the following week. I couldn't help thinking that it was too late already for me, not that I cared. God had let me down, and I wasn't worried on his account about my troubles. It was the way Mum looked. As they say in books, I had broken her heart. Then poor Bloody Jack, the best friend I ever had: even if he wasn't dead, he would have a terrible headache. I was sorry even for Dad, for he was so darn proud of the name of Sullivan that to have me a criminal would break his heart, too, if men's hearts did break. I wasn't sure about that.

I noticed my eyes were cracking up on me when we sat down and Sister Angela told us to get out our arithmetic books. Though arithmetic wasn't my best subject, I was quite glad at the idea of getting stuck into some figures, and opened my exercise book, flattening the pages out hard on the desk. I looked at the last work I had done, and there was my long division in a heck of a mess. The numbers ran into each other, and the whole sum tailed off to the edge of the page: at least, that's how it looked. I gave my head a shake, and darn me if the figures didn't bunch up and swing to the other side of the page. Then I realized that whatever was going to happen to me was on the way. I gripped my hands together and waited. I was glad it was happening here. The whole room around, with the holy pictures, and the rest of the kids, who were such decent birds, and Sister Angela, I liked her, too; the room with the walls, the two blackboards, the varnished wood benches, and Christ with his bleeding heart was the best picture of them all; old Joe Waters with his mother and father playing around the kitchen like that, and he always a great one for laughing at my jokes, and Sister Angela really not wanting to strap me and keen that I should grow up right; the room with the fireplace that didn't need a fire, the bunch of white flowers on the mantelpiece, with the traffic accident picture that the government had given the school pasted above; Legs Hope falling off his bike, and I'd lend him mine for a whole week if he wanted, and even Joseph Kane was decent enough in his way; Sister would know that it was as much God's fault as mine, if not more, because I had done my best, and he hadn't done a damn thing.

I closed my eyes and the terrible eyes of Mum looked at me, and then the dog's head flopped over, so I opened them again and stared at the clock with the red second hand that was on the shelf above Sister's desk. The hand jumped away from the face of the clock and began to swell and it ticked around in a bigger and bigger circle, fattening out like a big red balloon and getting nearer and nearer. All this was probably God creeping up on me, but I didn't care. I wasn't frightened. I sat there holding my hands together and thinking that no matter what happened I wasn't going to yell or scream. Or if I couldn't stand it any longer and had to cry out, as the red balloon got closer and closer, it would be, 'You bloody bastard' Then there was nothing but a warm floating red all around me and I lay back and drifted as though I was going off to sleep.

'Jimmy, Jimmy, Jimmy.' Sister Angela was nearly shouting when I woke up. Her face was hanging right over me, scared stiff under the flopping black veil, and she had an arm around my neck. I was flat out on the floor between the rows of desks. She was all jammed and doubled over to get at me. Her robes had a nice smell.

'Thank goodness, you're looking better,' she said. 'Would you be well enough to stand up, Jimmy?'

Her face was smack up against mine and the stiff starched white band that held her black veil away from her face had slipped back high on her head, and darn me if she didn't look as though she might be bald. I really meant to giggle, but the noise I made must have sounded like a snivel, for she said, 'Don't cry, Jimmy, you'll be all right.'

'I'm all right. I want to get up.'

She slipped her arm down around my shoulders, Joe's voice said, 'Let's all help, eh,' and about a dozen hands pushed and heaved at me. When I was up, my legs wobbled around. I hope nobody noticed.

The rest of the kids were crowding around, stretching their necks, and right at the back of the room Joseph Kane was standing on top of his desk to get a good view. Joe Waters said, 'I'll help, Sister,' and put his hand under my other shoulder. 'You look pretty sick, Jimmy,' he whispered. 'It must be something you ate or something.'

'We'll put you in my room,' said Sister, 'and you can have a rest.'

'I feel awfully sleepy,' I said.

Actually I was feeling so darn sleepy I didn't mind being taken into Sister's room—that was the place where she and Sister Bernice, who took the junior classes, had all their stuff; they even had a lavatory, too, shut off in one corner. We kids never really got a look in the room, and we didn't want to, either, as it seemed a little spooky.

Joe and Sister helped me to go through the other class-room, where all the kids must have stared at me—I don't remember noticing them, though—to the back of the school to the nun's room. As we went there was an almighty crash from behind us, and the whole school shook. Sister Angela said, 'Oh dear, what else would be happening?'

There was a couch in the room and I lay down on that. Joe said, 'You'll be as fit as a fiddle in two shakes of a lamb's tail,' and disappeared. I guessed he didn't much like coming all the way into there.

It was nearly dark, and so quiet, I felt all right, except for being tired—never in my life had I felt so tired.

'I think God's got it in for me, Sister,' I said as she put a blanket around me.

'Now, Jimmy, don't say that—God loves you as much as

148

anybody in the whole world. That doesn't mean he's not going to let you get sick now and then.'

I had my eyes open, but couldn't see much of her—only a black-and-white blur. And there was that nice smell as her robes were brushing over me as she pushed the edges of the blanket under my back. It was like moth balls and holy water mixed.

'It's more than that, Sister,' I said.

There was a cold wet smack on my cheek, and a noise like a cow pulling its legs out of a swamp. Sister had given me a thumping great kiss.

'Don't fret, Jimmy,' she said. 'The whole world will be better when you wake up.'

Then Joe's voice piped up from somewhere. 'Joseph Kane fell off the top of his desk, Sister. He's not hurt but Margie Flynn is crying with fright.'

Even the way I was I knew that Joe had been speaking to me, not to Sister. He had come all the way back to tell me that, because he knew it would give me a great kick. I stretched my eyes wide open to see him, so that I could wink or grin, but I could not find him. And the effort bunged up my eyes altogether, so I let them close, and that was that.

The next thing there was a lot of whispering. The voices were drifting around without words. My eyes were hurting, my mouth tasted like the bottom of a canary's cage, and my body was hot. I thought of saying, 'It's rude to whisper,' then I realized whoever it was that was doing the talking probably didn't want to wake me up. I lay there and tried to go back to sleep, so that I wouldn't be a nuisance.

I thought of how all the other kids would be talking about me. Now nothing would ever be the same again between them and I: sooner or later they would find out what I had done, and when Father Gilligan and Sister Angela knew, I would be sent away from the convent. Probably I would have to go to the public school in Kitchener Avenue, about a mile away, where all the Protestant children went. I had

149

never actually been friendly with Protestant kids, and it would be hard for me to have to live with them all day. But I could see that there was where I might be better off: Protestants were off side with God, and so was I. There might be kids at the public school who were even more off side than me, although it was unlikely. There had been some talk once about how some Protestant kid had hit his sister over the head with a fence post; if he was still going to school, I would probably have to sit next to him. Joe Waters and the rest of them wouldn't be able to speak to me, of course. If they did, it would be to yell, 'Proddy-hopper, proddy-hopper, go to hell.'

I didn't think that I would feel sorry for myself. I could work hard to grow up to be somebody like that Martin Luther, who did so much dirty work a long time ago. God wasn't going to have it both ways with me. Either he was on my side or I wouldn't be on his.

As I lay there on the couch dreaming away, it became so hot that in the end I had to kick the blanket off. There was a rustling from the darkness and I could barely make out Sister Angela standing over me.

'Are you awake now, Jimmy?' she said.

'It's dark,' I answered. 'I can't see anything.'

There was some more rustling, and then a blind behind the head of the couch went up with an awful rattle that nearly scared me out of my wits. I sat up and stared out the window. The sky was blue as billy-ho; the sun was shining as well as it could for winter; you could tell at a glance that anybody outside would be able to feel improved.

'You are looking so much better, bless you,' said Sister. 'Put your faith in God and remember never to stop praying, Jimmy. We'll all be praying for you, Jimmy, and God will help you.'

She was standing beside the window, and darn me she looked as though she had been crying. There were two wet patches starting under her eyes and running halfway down her cheeks, and the light made them show up like big pieces

150

of broken glass. And her voice was soft and full of breathing noises.

'I'm all right, Sister,' I said. 'That sleep did the trick.'

Just to prove it all to her, I stood up and stretched myself. I didn't feel as though I was likely to keel over again, and my legs didn't wobble, but I felt as though I was wrapped up in a big sheet of paper; I could see out, and yet there was this stuff between me and everything around.

'Is there going to be a lot of trouble, Sister?' I said. 'What will happen to me?'

She rushed over and gripped me by the wrist and said, 'Nothing will happen to you, Jimmy, if you trust in God.' That smooth face of hers was white as a sheet; she blinked away into my face, and her whisper was loud as a shout. 'Pray to the Holy Mother, Jimmy; pray to the Holy Mother. Now, with me.' She got down on her knees beside me, so I got down on mine and said a couple of Hail Mary's. I crossed myself and stood up, but she stayed on her knees, her hands clasping the hefty crucifix she always had stuck in her leather belt. She had to look up at me now, peering into my face as though she was trying to see if there were any signs of my sins there, and I couldn't help thinking how like my sister Molly she looked. Molly that time I found her flat on her back in the bedroom staring up at the roof. 'Don't worry, Sister,' I said. 'I'll be all right, I'll say my prayers, and I'll do my best to keep up with my schoolwork as well.' She grabbed me by the shoulders and pulled me up against her. 'God love you, boy,' she said, with her head against my chest. I was uncomfortable as heck, the way she held me, with the edge of her veil digging into my neck. Nevertheless, it did give me a kick to know that she was on my side, no matter what. If they put me in jail, I knew she would come and see me. For her sake I wouldn't let on about me and God.

Sister Angela got to her feet. 'Would you be well enough to come home with me now?' she asked. 'I've had our car come out so that you will be there in a minute.'

'What for, Sister? I'm all right, and it can wait until after school, can't it?' This talk about the car put the wind up me.

'Be patient, Jimmy. It has to be.'

The wrapped-up feeling got tighter. I was in for it, I knew. Poor old Bloody Jack was dead, or the Hindu had lost his eyes. I tried to think about that and couldn't. I couldn't think about a darned thing. Sister took me by the arm and led me out, and even the sun didn't make any difference to me. We walked around the back and up along the side of the building.

'I'm really very sorry I tore around here on my bike yesterday,' I said.

I looked at the walls of the school, made of great long strips of wood, and thought of the kids on the other side. They'd be pretty pleased with themselves because Sister wasn't with them, and at having no work to do. They were probably tossing darts around and flicking bent matches at each other with rubber bands. We got to one of the windows of our room, and Joe was staring out looking worried stiff. It was the only time I ever saw him with his mouth so closed up that his lips covered his teeth. When he saw me he didn't smile, but put his hand up to his shoulder, and then stuck one finger out and waggled it around. That was a secret signal which we used in gang wars and other games. It didn't mean anything except that we would watch out that nobody put anything across on the other.

Outside the gate was this blue car that looked as big as a bus. And on its luggage grid was tied my bike. Sister pushed me into the back seat and got in beside me, and I was staring at the back of the head of the man in the driver's seat. He didn't even look at us, this chap, just sat there, and as soon as we were in our seats he started the engine and away we went. He had a big black head and big shoulders with no neck in between. I didn't know much about cars, and had only ridden in one a few times, and then it wasn't a real car; it belonged to Mike Venutti, the fisher-

152

man, and he had cut all the back out of it and put a lorry tray there so he could carry loads of fish. It looked an awful mess, but it certainly could carry a pile of fish, and Mike didn't mind some of us kids riding on the back, too.

I was going to ask Sister Angela whose car this was, but when I turned to her I saw little bits of tears running down her face. Really, she looked a bit of a mess. Her lips were moving, and her hands were running over her rosary beads. It was no use getting mixed up in a conversation with her. I tried to sort out the whole business for myself, and only small bits of happenings would get together in my mind, and then they didn't fit together. Bloody Jack and the Hindu, of course, and my bike kept worrying me, or I'd see Mum falling down the stairs, Dad sitting on the chair in the kitchen looking happy in a funny way, and a red snake would wriggle across my eyes and turn into the second hand of the clock, and I began to feel cold. I knew this was the biggest of the big days: I thought of myself as Peter getting crucified upside down, or Saint Sebastian seeing the first arrows heading in his direction, and then changed my mind: I would be more like Lucifer getting tossed down to Hell.

As we turned up the road to home the ride became a little bumpy, and the car slowed down. Over the man's shoulder, through the windscreen, our house looked to me as though it was on a lopsided screen in a picture theatre, and the back seat of the car was so soft I could have been in the dress circle.

'I don't want to go home, Sister,' I said. As soon as the words were out I changed my mind, and said, 'Yes, I do.'

'I'll be with you all the time,' said Sister. 'It'll only by for a little time.'

We had arrived by then, and I didn't even bother to think why she should be there. For I could see a strange woman standing on our doorstep. She was fairly tall and thick, and she was beckoning to us as if we were to hurry.

153

20

NOTHING really bad had ever happened to me, unless you count having a tooth out or cutting a foot on a broken bottle. I had never really been knocked around; I daresay that bashing Bloody Jack gave me was the most I had ever been hurt. The dentist when he took my back tooth out certainly made me give an almighty yell, which scared the daylights out of him, and made a woman in the waiting room burst out crying, as though her tooth was coming out, too—the dentist got that much out of me, yet he didn't actually hurt. What caused me to yell was the crunching noise as he yanked. As I was only ten years old then, I thought for a minute that the side of my face was cracking off. So I yelled blue murder. When he got the tooth out he had to leave me straight away to go and fix the woman. I could hear her blubbing away, so I got out of the chair and poked my head into the waiting room before the nurse could stop me, and tried to tell her nothing awful had happened. Only my mouth got full of blood and I swallowed and choked on it and then heaved the whole lot out on to the carpet. The woman nearly had a fit and cleared out altogether. The dentist wasn't too pleased, and said if there were many more kids like me he would be driven out of business. Mum had left me there to go and do some shopping and when she came back the dentist told her that, too, although the nurse had cleaned up the blood and stuff by then, so the situation didn't look as bad as it had been.

There are still scars on the bottom of my right foot where I jumped on a broken bottle. That was years ago now, so the cuts must have been pretty bad. And that didn't hurt so very much; it was more the idea that my foot might be worse than it looked that upset me. That was a time Molly was home. We were home by ourselves for the afternoon, and she tore up a practically whole bed sheet and bound my foot and my leg up to the knee. She kept tying the strips around and around, so business-like and fussy and looking so proud that I let her go ahead because I could see that she was quite pleased with me for having the accident.

When I say that nothing really bad happened to me, I am thinking of things like that. I was pretty lucky there. I mention this so that it doesn't appear that I am moaning all the time. On the other hand, I do think I had awfully bad luck with the type of things that don't hurt your body but just worry you stiff. And if I had my choice, I would rather have had my leg broken once or twice, or an eye knocked out, or even got polio.

Perhaps a kid who has had such things go wrong with him would think I was better off, so there's no telling, really.

But when I got out of the car with Sister Angela and saw that woman beckoning to us, it was worse than a broken leg could ever be. She in this costume like a sack and with one hand on her hip standing on top of the steps looking as though she owned the place. She had a face like half-cooked meat. I have never hated anybody in my life as much as I hated her. As soon as I saw her I wanted to kick her to pieces or stamp on her till she screamed.

'What's she doing here, Sister?' I asked.

Sister Angela put her arm around my shoulder and said, 'Come along with me, Jimmy, and be a brave boy,' and sort of pushed me on down the path.

'Where's my mother?' I said, and my voice zigzagged around so much I felt ashamed.

The woman said, 'Is he all right?'

'Yes,' Sister said.

She had brown shoes on and thick brown stockings and was more like a man. A man who played football. She reached back and opened the door and stood there with one hand out and said, 'Come on in, then. You won't be able to keep him here for very long. I think it's a mistake, but she wouldn't lift a finger until we promised.'

'You get out of here,' I said to her. 'This is not your house and you can just get out of it.'

And then Sister was on her knees beside me, right on the gravel, dropping straight down without hitching or messing with her robes, her hand on my shoulder scratching away as though she thought I might be itching. 'Jimmy, you must be a brave boy and you must be a good boy. I'll stay with you all the while. I'm taking you in to see your mother. Please be a brave and a good boy.' Her voice was zigzagging, too.

'Couldn't I go down to the police station?' I said. 'What's it to do with her, anyway? This is not her house. She can't come hanging around here because I've got into trouble, can she?'

'She's here to help, Jimmy. She's here to help your mother. And you'll never go to the police station.'

'They're going to put me in jail, aren't they?'

There was a clop-clop down the stairs and the woman crouched down with her red-and-brown face up against mine, and said, 'Your mummy told me to come out and watch for you. I'm your mummy's friend, see. Nothing's going to happen to you because you are a good little boy, see, and the police never touch good little boys.'

'I want to see my mother,' I yelled at them.

That did it. Even the woman shut up. They both tapped me up the steps with their hands and followed me across the porch and up the passage. The kitchen door was open and I saw all the unwashed breakfast dishes on the sink, and the teapot standing on the table with its lid off, and the stove fire out. I stopped, but the woman tapped me forward again, and said, 'Your mother is waiting for you in the lounge.'

'Keep away from me, all of you,' I said, and ran up the passage, pulled the door open, ducked in, and slammed it behind me. Mum was leaning right back in the big chair, and must have been nearly asleep, for she sat up with a jerk. She was still the same only her eyes weren't so queer. But her face was white and those funny lines were all sagging over it; she looked as though she had too much skin.

'It's all because of me, isn't it?' I said. 'It's my fault, isn't it?'

She held out her arms. I went across and she gave me a hug that squeezed the breath out of me, at the same time rubbing her face across the top of my head so hard it nearly hurt.

'I'm sorry, son. Remember that when you grow up.' She whispered that as she pushed me away from her again.

'I wouldn't be surprised if I've got cancer or some whopping tropical fever,' I said. 'It's all happened because I was sick, Mum. They can't blame me because I was sick. My brain was all mucked up.'

'Jimmy, don't talk like that.'

'I fainted at school, Mum. Honest. Bang over I went. Sister'll tell you.'

'Don't gabble away like that, son,' she said, not even caring.

'But the Hindu and Bloody Jack, Mum.' I did my best to talk slow. 'It wasn't really my fault, not if I'm sick and have to be operated on, even if I did swear at that old woman over the fence.'

'Your father's gone away, son. That's what I want to tell you. I've got to go, too. You'll have to live with the sisters at a convent for a while.'

'What?' I sort of hiccupped over her. Honestly, I had been so steamed up about the idea of being in trouble that I didn't hear right the first time, so she repeated herself. It was like the time I learned the wrong oral spelling lesson off by heart, and then got flattened properly when Sister asked me to spell conceit. Mum was staring at me, still looking as though she hadn't had any sleep for a year, and talking to me about something I had never dreamed of. I just stood there as though my tongue was in a knot.

157

'You'll stay in a convent like Molly, Jimmy,' she said.

Even now, I can hear her talking, and remember every word she said, even what I said myself, and at nights before I go to sleep I often listen to it over and over again. I suppose because at the time I didn't feel much, or understand, and I'm still trying to catch up, so to speak.

'Where's Dad gone?' I asked her.

'He's gone, that's all. Don't ask me. There's a new job, that's it, and he has gone away for that, a long, long way away. You'll understand when you grow up, Jimmy. I'm sorry.'

'I don't want to go anywhere, Mum. Not without you and Dad.'

'I don't want to leave you, either, Jimmy. I have to, though, you see. We all have to do things we don't want to do. I'm sorry. You're a big boy now, aren't you? I'll get back soon and take you, and perhaps you and Molly and me, all three of us, will go somewhere else.'

'Why somewhere else?'

'We don't live in one place all our lives. Please don't ask questions. Say you'll be a good boy and pray for Mummy.'

'Where's Dad?'

'I told you where he is, son. Please don't ask questions. I'll give you sixpence and you can buy yourself an ice cream on the way to the home. There'll be other children in the home, and the sisters will look after you.'

'Where did he go, and why didn't he say good-bye to me?'

'To a new job, a long way away, I told you. He left early. I've put all the clothes you'll need in a case, and the rest of your gear will be sent on after you, and in a little while Mummy will come for you and we'll go away together. It won't be long, either. You'll like living in the home with all the other boys and girls. It's not far from Wellington. Molly will come out to see you.'

'I don't want to go. I won't.'

'Jimmy, Jimmy, you'll like it fine. Can't you see it has

to be? Mummy doesn't want you to go away. It's not my fault, son. I have done my best. I'll be thinking of you all the time. It's not my fault. I tried to put up with so many terrible things, things you'll never know, and it's not my fault, God knows. I couldn't stand it any longer, Jimmy, and nobody will blame me when they know.'

'What are you talking about, Mum?'

She stood up and walked over to the fireplace. She put both her hands on the mantelpiece and said, 'Be a good boy, won't you, son?'

'I am a bit bad, I suppose, but not that bad,' I said.

From upstairs came a bumping sound, and then feet trampled around. Mum put her hand on the little brass statue of the fat Chinaman and rattled it on the mantelpiece. The thumpings went on, and she didn't move, just stood there, as though she would never be able to speak again. I didn't give a darn about the house, really, yet everything in that lounge seemed to be worth a heck of a lot, even the bare old carpet, the old writing bureau with the wriggling carvings, all the stuff, even the old junk that was in there, including that picture of the whopping big stag; honestly, I've never felt anything was worth that much, not even piles of five-pound notes, and here I was getting the feeling about stuff I wouldn't have given you twopence for the day before. Then the bumping stopped and there was no noise except the rattle of the fat Chinaman.

'What's happened, Mum? Who's upstairs?'

She turned around and faced me, and her face was starting to screw up as if she was wild. 'Don't ask any more questions, Jimmy,' she said. 'I've told you all a little boy needs to know. You'll have to go now.'

'Don't you worry about me being sick with disease and fainting,' I blubbed at her. 'You can't let them put me in jail.'

'Nobody is going to put you in jail. Don't talk nonsense, son. Only go with Sister and I'll see you soon. It won't be long.'

I stopped being me then: the mad feeling that I had when I started throwing stones the day before blew up inside me. 'What are you doing to me?' I shouted as she came toward me with her arms stretched out. I closed my eyes and the shout came again, 'What are you doing to me?' and then she had lifted me right off my feet and was saying, 'Quiet, quiet, please, please, please.' I was held like that for a long time, and she kept repeating 'please, please' until another hand pulled at my shoulder and the voice of the woman said very loudly, 'Time is getting on, Mrs Sullivan. Only a few minutes, that was our agreement, wasn't it?'

'I'll come for you soon, Jimmy,' Mum said. Her arms loosened around me and I slid down her legs till my feet were on the floor.

'It's nearly midday,' the woman said.

I put my arms around Mum's waist and held my face there.

'Oh, my God, what have I done to deserve all this?' she said.

'Remember our agreement,' the woman said. 'I told you what would happen.'

They were Mum's hands that came behind her back and pulled my hands away and then took my wrists and lifted my arms right up above my head and level with her shoulders. I didn't look at her, just held my arms stiff.

'Don't be silly, son,' she said, and then mumbled something I couldn't hear.

The woman's hands took my arms, so I let them drop. I stared at the floor all the time.

'Good-bye, Jimmy,' Mum said.

'Say good-bye to your mother and I'll take you out to the nun,' said the woman.

Mum's hands were on my shoulders now, and she leaned on them as she bent down and kissed me on the forehead. I started to look up and saw the long red scratch on her arm again and my neck was so stiff that I couldn't move my head. I couldn't look at her.

'Good-bye son,' Mum said. 'Be a brave man.'

'He'll be all right, Mrs Sullivan,' the woman said. And then right against my ear she went on, 'Don't sulk, sonny. Say good-bye to your mother.'

'Oh, my God,' said Mum, sounding as though her mouth couldn't open properly.

I turned right around into the sack of the woman's skirt and pushed past her, and there at the door was the black robe of Sister Angela and splitting down the middle of it were the rosary beads hanging from the crucifix at her waist. I walked over and Sister's hand touched my cheek.

'Good-bye, Mum,' I said.

'Good-bye, Jimmy,' she said from behind me.

I couldn't look at her, though, and went on out into the passage. Sister Angela whispered, 'Down to your room, Jimmy.' Why Mum had been so terrible to me I didn't know: there she was back in that lounge with that woman, somebody I had never even seen before, and neither of them wanted me. The whole house was cold and dusty and creaking, as though it was filling up with ghosts, while I was being shovelled out of the way as quickly as possible. The sun was beating in the open front door and its light was shooting up the passage making dust in the air look like little bits of fire. Yet it was cold. And Sister Angela looked frightened and her mouth was moving like a rabbit's eating grass. 'Down to your room, Jimmy,' she said again as I stood, looking around. She took my hand and held it tightly, yet she didn't move, either. There were more bumps upstairs; this time I could tell they were footsteps. From somewhere about us there was a moaning, almost like a dog howling, that faded as soon as it started and then stopped. It stopped, yet I knew it was still going on—only nobody was being allowed to hear it. I tugged Sister's hand and led her down to my room, not caring, and said to her, 'Leave me alone, leave me alone, everybody leave me alone.' She stepped back, nodding her head. 'In a minute we'll go, Jimmy. I'll tell them we are ready to leave.' She could hardly speak, really; I felt sorry for her. I was tougher than she was.

She closed the door as she went out. My bed hadn't been made, so I pulled the blankets halfway up, shook the pillow out, smoothed it down, and then settled the blankets right to the top of the bed, over the pillow. The top blanket was thick and covered with black-and-red lines that made up squares, so I was careful to straighten it so that the squares were all in line. There was an open suitcase on the floor at the foot of the bed, which I pulled out to the centre of the room. I couldn't help noticing that Mum had packed my clothes any old way, so I tidied up the pyjamas and shirts on top, in case anybody at the home noticed. There was a chest of drawers next to my bed and I checked in each drawer to make sure nothing was forgotten that I really wanted. There was a fair amount of my junk in the bottom drawer, but I only took an old hourglass in a wooden frame that I had found years before in a rubbish tip. I timed it once and the sand ran from one end to the other in fifty minutes. Anyway, I stuffed it down into the bottom of the case, closed the lid and snapped the locks and then sat on top of it. My bedroom was a neat room, with not much in it besides the bed and chest of drawers, which Dad had whitewashed the same time as he had the lounge walls, a mirror that was cracked in one corner where I hit it with the hair-brush I had thrown at a white butterfly that had flown in the window (funny, Mum never noticed that crack), a little table that rocked when you put your elbows on it, and an old chest in which I kept all my books. There were a couple of holy pictures on the walls, too, not that I really wanted them there—when I was seven or eight I was keen on the Virgin Mary and stuck one picture of her on each side of the room, and I had never actually felt like taking them down again, even though I didn't really want them up there any longer. It was a good room, yet I didn't feel sorry that I was leaving it; even thinking about the mousehole in the corner where I used to stuff my bag of marbles didn't make me get sloppy. I sat on my suitcase, half dreaming until I slowly started to wake up. My heart began to thump and it began to get hard for me to breathe. I went across to the window. The sun was bright and the bit of a lawn in front dry and warm, and two cars were parked on the road. Two cars. One was the one that had brought me home with Sister Angela, and the other was a long black job, bigger than any car I had ever seen. I shoved my face up hard against the window and looked out at an angle. There was a policeman standing on the path. He moved out a bit, slowly at first, looking back over his shoulder and moving his lips as though he was talking to somebody. His hands were the size of footballs, and the tops of his arms were bursting tight against his sleeves, making them look as though they were pumped tight with air, and he had no neck at all: there were two or three great rings of red fat under his chin that hid his collar, and then his shoulders bunched out like thundering great hills that had come up from his waist. He didn't have a fat belly, either, and his legs were long. He was all muscles and beef up top and only average down below.

He finished talking and then walked up the path and through the gate, and untied my bike from the back of the car. He was so strong that he lifted it up in the air and lowered it to the ground with one hand on the bar. And then he pushed it back down the path with two fingers resting on the middle of the handle bars.

Really, my mind had not been working at all well because it was not till I saw the policeman with that bike that I realized that all the trouble was not about what I had done the day before. It was something about Mum and Dad.

21

I WAS glad. The glad feeling was the greatest I've ever felt in my whole life. It didn't last long, yet while it was there I shivered, leaning against the window, pressing the side of my face against the glass; I shivered from head to foot, so glad that I wanted to run and jump around the lawn. That was the Devil in me, I daresay: even though Mum was looking like a sick old woman and Dad had gone away. I was still glad it was not me that was in trouble.

That only lasted a second, and then I felt worse than ever. But the point is, I did feel glad. Then all the pictures tumbled up in my mind of Dad turning back to the house when I told him about our not having enough money to buy me a bike: his face kept showing up in front of mine and it was looking as mad as a March Hare; then it was his back as he walked away from me, his arm jiggling up and down. And there was another picture of Mum on her hands and knees on the path, looking at me as though she wanted to crawl away; then she was old and criss-crossed with deep lines, and her eyes were so far back into her head that there were just dark patches where they should have been.

I wanted to go back to Mum and hold on to her and never let her go. They'd have to kill me to send me away from her again, I thought: I would hold on so tight and she would hold on to me.

I jumped back from the window and grew dizzy as everything began to shrink, like a piece of darned bacon frying. The red-and-black blanket on my bed looked like a handkerchief, and my suitcase in the middle of the floor a tiny purse. Then the walls and the roof pressed in, and it seemed that all I had to do was put out my hand and open the door to get to Mum. I was so big I didn't have to walk across the room. And the door opened, and now I did move my feet out to the passage. Right ahead of me were the big black robes of Sister Angela and the brown sack costume of the woman: they were huge. I had to stare up at the back of their heads, which went way up past the ceiling into the sky, except that the sky wasn't there. Sister's head was covered in a veil that looked like a black circus tent, and the woman had hair that looked like a huge pile of hanging ropes.

Sister's voice was shouting. If it had come through a radio going full blast, it couldn't have been louder. 'I'll see how he is tomorrow. He'll have to know sometime, and it would only be right that he knows that his father is dead. That's all he need know. We'll leave the rest in God's hands. Letters from his mother will help as long as she can write them.'

That woman screamed: 'It will all be left to you. It is good that he is being taken away at once, because the whole village will know.'

Sister shouted, 'Oh, his poor mother, may God have mercy on her.'

They moved away together and I stepped back until I was level with the bedroom door, and then I shuffled sideways until I was looking down on my small bed, and all the time Sister's voice was blazing away 'his father is dead', over and over again. I felt too big and it seemed too far away for me to try and lie down on the bed, and as the floor seemed to be all right under my feet, I let myself go to my knees, and then I lay down sideways and rolled over on my back. The top of my head pushed against something hard, so I put up my hand and pushed. It was my case and it was heavy. Even while the voice was still going on I could still think that if the case was still heavy it couldn't be so small and that meant that I couldn't really be so big. I must be having a queer spell, I thought, only this one is the worst ever and I'm dying.

Then the voice stopped and the pictures started again. Dad was there in his best dark suit with a white collar and blue tie, and his face was clean and shining as if he had just finished shaving. He was holding out his arm. 'Dad,' I called. I opened my eyes and there was the ceiling above me. It was the same as it had always been. By twisting my head I could see that the whole room was the way it had always been: it wasn't big any more. I was the same too. Old Jimmy Sullivan, flat out on his back in his bedroom, like his silly sister Molly had been that time. And then away I went.

My heart began to get cracking again, bumping at my ribs until my whole body was shaking. I rolled over and pushed myself up to my feet. I stood stock-still, waiting for the air to have a go at me. I made up my mind that God was really going to scrag me this time, and I wouldn't even bother to fight back. He could do what he darned well liked because it didn't really matter any longer. The air got colder and colder, all right, and thicker and thicker. I could have started shovelling it around like ice cream. Then it got like the marble stuff and started to lie on my arms and legs, making them heavy, and then it worked up over my throat and under my chin and slowly tightened up as if it was going to choke me. My heart gave a really awful backfire and I lost my nerve. My legs moved, all right, as I headed out the door, slamming it back with my hands that were awfully heavy. If I had been up to my neck in mud it couldn't have felt any tougher to move up the passage. I had both hands on the wallpaper on one side and sort of slithered forward. I was moving darn quickly even though I felt as though I weighed a ton, and my throat was choked and my chest heaved up and down. All I could think of was getting to the bathroom for my protection trick before it was too late. The bathroom door was open and I fell through it with a bang and it hurt my shoulders to lift my arms and pull myself up over the edge of the bath itself so I could turn on the hot-water tap. There were clouds of steam, and I knew that the water must be boiling but I

166

didn't care. I spouted out 'Hail Mary, full of grace,' and so on, because now the marble was on top of my head and filling in my ears, and propped both my arms out. Funny, I'm sure there was no feeling at first, for I was on the 'blessed is the fruit of thy womb' part when the back of my hands and wrists caught fire. It used to be a game with us kids to get magnifying glasses and spot the sun through them on to our skin to see how long we could stand the burn. That made only a little pinpoint of hurting to what hit me now. At first I didn't want to pull my arms back, even though I screamed my head off, and then when the burning got deeper I didn't seem to be able to shift them, as my arms wouldn't darn well move. The pain spread all over my body and I let myself fall sideways and kept on screaming. There was nothing but steam around me and I thought the Devil must have his hands on my arms and be pulling me down to Hell. And when the eyes and cheek bones of this face came pushing down on top of me, I was sure it was a Hindu devil and screamed at him to leave me alone. I remember shouting 'It wasn't my fault, it wasn't' as he got closer. The face said, 'God love you, boy, what are you doing to yourself?' and became Father Gilligan. I suppose it was Father Gilligan all the time, but the first face I saw had slanting eyes that were glaring mad; Father's face is thin, and what a wonder I didn't see his big nose straight away. He lifted me up off the floor with his hands under my armpits, and then pushed me up over his shoulder and hugged me to him. We were out the back door in no time at all. I can't even remember going, in fact, until we were outside and my hands and wrists hurt again so badly that I yelled. Sister Angela was about somewhere, for she was crying, 'I only left him alone for a few minutes.' My chin bounced on Father Gilligan's shoulder and he pushed me farther up so that I was nearly flopping down his back, with my arms hanging down in front of me. I was blubbing like a baby all the time, I don't mind admitting, and I opened my eyes only once. Even in all the hurting, it came to me as I bounced around on Father's shoulder that I was being taken away from home, so I opened my eyes and took a quick look back before my hands made me cry again. All I saw was that big policeman standing at the back of the house holding that bike and staring at me.

22

MOLLY wrote me sloppy letters about how I was not to worry, and how we must stick together, and how she would help me. But she didn't come to see me until after a couple of months had gone. All that time I was here, not knowing exactly what had happened to me, in this convent, a whacking big wooden building covered with fire escapes in the middle of some grounds in the middle of the country. It's a long way from Raggleton and a long way from the sea, and once you get out of the grounds there's nothing much except farms with sheep and cows mooching around. We have our own cows here, incidentally, and I'm in the milking gang every other night. I can drag my share out of the old girls with the best of them.

But about Molly. All the nuns thought it was a great event, her coming, and they fussed and flapped around. They had a cup of tea and hot scones waiting for her in Sister Francis's room and kept telling me how wonderful it all was, what with Molly having to catch a train all the way from Wellington, and then catch the mail car and come· all that way to see her little brother. Sister Theresa, who is not much more than knee-high to a grasshopper, got a scissors and comb out the night before and cut my hair to blazes and darn near hacked my ear off. Every time she made a mistake, all she said was 'hen feathers'.

In the morning, they had me out of bed and into a bath, made me polish my shoes extra hard, and Sister Francis actually stood there shaking and watched me while I cleaned my teeth. Then I had a clean shirt on, and my pants were pressed and Sister Theresa pulled my socks up to below my knees. When I heard about them having a cup of tea ready for Molly it really made me sick. I had been looking forward to seeing Molly, but they just knocked it all out of me, so I stood outside the main gates waiting for the mail car with Sister Theresa, not really giving a damn, and thinking it wouldn't upset me if she didn't turn up. When the car came around the bend, though, I felt glad somehow and more than anything else in the world I wanted to see Molly, although I wasn't going to be such a fool as to let on.

'I'll leave you here so you can meet your sister all by yourself like a grownup man,' Sister said, full of beans, and then skipped around and bolted back down the drive like a shot out of a gun.

Molly was in the seat beside the driver. She poked her head and shoulders out the window as the car stopped. It was awful, because for a second she looked like Mum did that last morning. Well, she didn't actually look like Mum, but there was something the same as Mum about her. She looked as though she had a really bad cold, only she didn't. Her eyes had bits of red in them, her face was skinny-looking, and her lips were shrivelled up into lots of tiny cracks. She didn't smile at me, either, at first. She looked at me terribly hard. Now that I think of it, I suppose I was looking at her just as hard, too.

'Hello, big boy,' she said. 'Long time no see.' Then she smiled, improving her looks tremendously.

'Hello, Molly,' I said. 'How are you?'

'I'm fine. How are you?'

'I'm O.K.'

The mailman, one of those jokers who always looks busy, skedaddled around the side of the car, gave me the mailbag, and ducked back again as though he were running a race. Molly got out of the car as he was getting back and he called after her, 'Don't forget to be here at eleven sharp, Miss Brown.' Then he roared off.

'He's got your name wrong,' I said.

There was no doubt that Molly was a grownup even more now. I could see that as she stood there. She had one of those brown costumes on that have a skinny skirt

170

with a jacket that doesn't come much below the armpits, over a white shirt. The funny thing about this shirt was that the collar didn't lie down: it stood straight up and darn near banged into her ears. She didn't have a hat on and her hair was pulled as flat as a pancake back on her head. What with her high heels she looked like one of these women in the magazines who stand around holding a glass in their hands.

'What about a kiss for your big sister?' she said, putting her arms around my shoulders and giving me a hug. She had a handbag in one hand and a brown-paper parcel in the other and these dug into my back as she landed one on my nose.

'You're looking a bit run-down in the face but apart from that you're not looking too bad,' I said.

'It's ages since we last saw each other, Jimmy.'

'Yes,' I said.

'You've no idea how glad I am to see you. You're looking so well, I'm so pleased, and my, you're growing up. You are going to be big, Jimmy, which is very good for a man.'

'Thanks,' I said, as we turned to walk to the convent. 'Have you stopped growing by now? I see your chest is still sticking out pretty well and your tummy isn't bulging.'

That made her give one of her old giggles. She tucked the parcel under her arm, and with her free hand banged me on the back of the neck. She didn't say anything, and suddenly I felt happier than I had been for a long time. It wasn't that I thought Molly was wonderful; it was just that she was somebody connected with me, if you know what I mean.

Of course, the sisters made a great fuss over her. When they dished out the tea they gave me a cup and I even managed to clean up a couple of the scones, too, so it turned out quite well. Sister Francis and Sister Theresa were with us. All the talk was about me, practically, how I was doing my school-work well, how good I was, and all that sort of stuff. I had to admire Molly, the way she sat there, sipping away at her tea like Lady Muck, looking so darned earnest, really holding up her own end of the stick. The more I looked at her face the more I could see how she had changed. She was still good to look at, even beautiful, as they say, and her features were the same, yet there was this difference. For instance, her eyes were as blue as ever, yet you couldn't see very far into them; they were steamed up like a bathroom window. And her lips didn't only have the dents in them—they bent down at the corners.

'Jimmy can't take his eyes off you, he's so happy to see you,' said Sister Theresa.

Anyway, by the time all the messing around and talking was finished it was ten o'clock, and then she said, 'Oh, you'd like to show Molly around the convent, wouldn't you, Jimmy? Off the two of you go together. You haven't much time.'

Outside, it was getting hot. Even though the sun was behind all the clouds in the sky it was still going well. It was nearly summer again, of course, and even though I missed the sea, I was beginning to see that the country wasn't too bad at such a time. I said to Molly, 'You don't really want to see the old convent, do you?' and led her over to the bench under the acorn tree next to the orchard. She trailed along behind as though I was the boss and together we sat down.

'I'm still worried about your face,' I said. 'I'm not being cheeky, but it does seem a bit mucked up, not that there's anything wrong with it, really.'

That really wasn't what I wanted to talk about. But I had to say something.

'Did you mind terribly, Jimmy?' she said. 'About Mum and Dad. I want you to know everything's all right and I'll look after you when you leave here.'

Old Molly wasn't like Lady Muck any more. She dropped her face right down as she spoke and her ears nearly disappeared under that funny collar, it pushed so far up.

'Everybody here has a mother and father dead. They

172

are worse off than me,' I said. 'I don't know why Mum doesn't come to see me though. She doesn't ask me to come and see her, either. I don't know why she doesn't want to see me. I want to see her.'

'She can't honestly. She is sick in a kind of a way that makes doctors keep others away. I can go and see her and, oh, Jimmy, she is . . .'

'What is she then?' I said.

'The only thing that worries her is that she can't see you. She asks me to tell you that she loves you, and that she is thinking of you all the time.'

'She writes to me and tells me to be good and all that but she never says anything about wanting to see me, except in her first letter.'

Molly wheeled around on the bench and pushed her face close to mine and said, 'She can't, Jimmy. That's what she wants me to explain to you. That's all you ask her in your letters and she wants me to make you understand. She didn't write about it because she knew I would explain, that's why.'

'Don't get on your high horse,' I said.

She shut her eyes, kissed me on the cheek, grabbed my hands and squeezed them, and then half hugged me up against her.

'Your chest is sticking into me,' I said.

She let us get unstuck again and tossed off a big sigh, 'I really don't understand you, old chap.'

'That's all right for you to talk, because you're grown up. I'm out here and I don't even see Mum. They just tell me she's in a hospital and that God knows best and all that shit, just like about Dad, and nobody even knows anything about me and all the time I'm the only one that knows. They were my mother and father more than they were your mother and father because you weren't even there but I was. I was there all the time with them while you were having a great old time down in Wellington. I was with them and I'm the only one that knows.' I was doing

173

my block again, of course, and seeing her look frightened out of her wits didn't stop me either.

'You didn't even like them,' I went on at her. 'You even said you weren't going to come back home and you were always turning up your nose at them. I don't know why Mum doesn't let me see her. It isn't fair. Put that in your pipe and smoke it.'

She brushed away at her skirt, bending down over her lap as though she were looking for crumbs from the scones she had eaten. There was stamping in the orchard and a flapping of wings as a couple of the pet lambs we kept there chased in among the hens. Out on the road the milk truck clanged along; the driver waved as he saw us under the tree. Back at the convent a window slammed open and a couple of the kids started talking until somebody called to them and the window was closed again. While all this went on Molly kept brushing away at her skirt, leaving me to sit on my hands.

'I'm sorry, old chap,' she said at last. 'Perhaps it is something we shouldn't talk about. You remember that Mum told me to tell you. I don't blame you for being wild with me, really I don't, except that I wouldn't like you to be too hard on me. Remember that there are lots of things that you mightn't understand. Perhaps I had all sorts of terrible things to put up with, things that you know nothing about, although I'm not saying I did—but if I did, that would make a difference, wouldn't it?'

'What are you brushing away at your skirt for, anyway?'

'You've made me nervous, that's why. Talking like that, and where did you learn that awful word you used a minute ago?'

'That one? It means cow dung. It's not that bad. Anyway, I'm sorry. After all, you did come all the way out to see me and I'm glad to see you. Don't worry about me and Mum and Dad, as I'll be all right. Lots of kids have no fathers and don't see their mothers.'

'That's right, Jimmy. You are very sensible.'

174

'It's not too bad Dad having an accident like that, falling down and hitting his head, as lots of people have accidents. They get killed in cars, in railway trains, in aeroplanes, in tractors, in water—accidents are happening all the time.'

'You're lucky, old boy. You don't know how lucky you are.'

'And with Mum sick, that's only natural, husbands and wives being what they are. I don't mind her not seeing me, not really.'

Poor old Molly was looking sad as blazes, almost as though she was going to heave up her tea and scones. I began to feel like her big brother now.

'You know something,' I said. 'Mum and Dad were very happy, laughing and kissing each other. Dad once picked Mum up in the kitchen and twirled her around, even though he only had one arm. They were mugging each other all the time as though they were in Hollywood, you know. They had a bath together once, there. Mum was in the bath and Dad jumped in with her, that's how friendly they were. So when Dad got killed like that it's no wonder Mum got sick.'

'Yes,' Molly said.

Really, she looked a proper sap, sitting there. The nearest I could describe her would be to say that she reminded me in some ways of a kid in this convent who wets his pants pretty regularly. When he does it in class he just sits there rolling his eyes as though the world has come to an end.

Anyway, I had Molly licked from then on; she didn't try to talk to me any more about Mum and Dad. We yarned about the convent and she told me about this lawyer's office in Wellington where she was working, and how nice everybody was to her there. I told her that I didn't see why she should be surprised at that, but she couldn't see my point. I was to stay on at the convent till I was sixteen, and then I was to come and live with Mum and her, if Mum was out of the hospital. I told her I was quite happy about that, and I was, because even then I could see that I would need an education before I took off on my own. I kidded Molly some more, reminding her what she had told me at the beach that time and asking her if some old rich man was going to marry her. That made her blush. While we were on the subject, I asked her if it was true about what men and women did—some of the older kids were talking about it even here—and whether she had tried it for herself yet. This made her even worse, and when she told me off I asked her if she expected me to find out from the nuns. She said no, that I should wait until I came to live with her in Wellington and she would see I read the right books because the subject was very technical. Actually, I was only making conversation, and didn't really give a darn.

Nothing much else happened between me and Molly. We walked about the convent grounds a bit before she went back to say good-bye to the nuns, and then we went out to the gate and waited for the mail car. She gave me the brown-paper parcel as a present—it was a book, *The Three Musketeers*—kissed me again, and away she went, and I haven't seen her since. About the only thing I remember was that the busy mailman said to her as she got in the car, 'Thanks for being on time, Miss Brown.' I was closing the door behind her and was about to tell him her name was Sullivan when she gave me a look that somehow or other stopped me.

23

I SHOULDN'T complain, I suppose, as I'm alive and kicking, and there's not much doubt that I'm tougher and smarter than most boys my age. I don't care what else God is going to try on me, but whatever it is, he had better watch his step. Anyway, I've got this feeling that came over me when Sister Francis told me a few weeks after Molly came that Mum would be in the hospital a long time, and that I wouldn't be able to see her for years and years, that's how sick she was. I didn't blubber or anything like that. I just sat there while she talked. Her office is a bare old room with her only desk and a row of bookcases behind stacked high with papers and books. There's nothing on the walls, not a darned thing, except this big crucifix. She's pretty dried-up to look at, is Sister Francis, and she actually has the shakes; her hands wobble ever so slightly, and her head nods up and down; as they say about boxers who are getting on in years, she is over the hill. But she's a good old thing, and God can do no wrong as far as she is concerned.

Well, I listened away to her and, though I might have pulled a face, I didn't let on about how I felt. After a while she got up and asked me if I would like to go for a walk with her, so we went down the corridor and out the back door. We walked through the vegetable gardens, and this being early November everything was fairly kicking it along, the cabbages and silver beet and stuff particularly. As I said, Sister is pretty ancient, and once we were on the clay road behind the convent, she took my hand and said, 'You won't mind helping me a little, Jimmy, will you? There are holes in the road and I would like to have some support in case I trip.' I took a firm grip on her hand and nodded, and away we went, dawdling along, so that she wouldn't get winded.

It was funny that the news about Mum didn't hit me the way Dad's death did. When they first brought me here I stayed in bed doing nothing but cry for days. It wasn't because my hands were hurting, either. They had a doctor fix the burns up straight away, although it took months for them to really heal. For a while there I must have been nearly off my rocker. Then one morning I woke up and it was all over. Just before I opened my eyes I thought of how Dad used to say you couldn't keep a Sullivan down, and how he was going to see that I had a better chance than he did: the way he put it sometimes was silly, of course; but he did mean what he said, and I always felt he thought I was somebody pretty good. And there was Mum, always so keen to have me spick and span and looking well, and always doing her best for me; she was proud of me, too. As I said, all this was in my mind just before I opened my eyes, and somehow or other it hit me so that I sat right up in bed, hungry enough to eat a horse, and wanting to show everybody that I was as good as anybody else, if not better.

That was nearly two years ago. Molly really had the laugh on me in the end, I have to hand her that. About three months after she had come to see me, she skipped her usual weekly letter and darn me if about a fortnight went by before I heard from her. Then this letter came with a stamp carrying a picture of a kangaroo sitting on his backside. Molly wrote that she was married to the most wonderful man in the world and he had taken her to live in Sydney, where he was building her a wonderful house by some beach. In other letters since then, she tells me that he is an old rich man, which is a smack in the eye for me. I never dreamed a man of thirty-five would be interested in a silly girl like Molly. And this chap must be extremely clever, as he runs a whole airline. If I decide to be a pilot when I grow up it shouldn't be too hard for me to get a start.

Mum writes to me, too, not saying much, really, and

nothing at all about the hospital, of course, except odd little things that don't fool me. I try to write long letters to her, yet often after getting to the bottom of one page it is hard to think of something else to start another with: I would like to tell her that I know, and that she doesn't have to worry, but that would make it hard for her. So we both are fooling each other, except that I'm not fooled, really. I know she killed Dad.

Nobody else wrote to me, not even Joe Waters, excepting Bloody Jack. He sent a note in a dirty old letter addressed to me, '*care of R.C. Sisters, Raggleton Convent,*' and Sister Angela posted it on to me. '*I'm very sorry I hit you that day on the wharf because I might have known.*' said Jack. '*There's not much fish as usual. I bet it was you breaking the Hindu's window, he wasn't hurt much. I would have helped you if you had told me, and I hope you are still a friend of old Jack's. There's a lot of new railway stuff here for frozen meat and it is all painted a funny kind of red.*' He signed it, '*Yrs, Jack Crannery,*' which was the first I knew of his name. I didn't write back to him, because he didn't give any address and what was the use, anyway.

As for Joe Waters and the rest of them, I understand, all right. They're still my friends, yet they wouldn't know what to say in a letter. Neither would I, so it's better all round that we don't try.

So now I often think of my mother and father, not really caring. Most nights I go to sleep hearing them talking. It is not all bad, either: sometimes they are alone with me and I am hearing again the good times there used to be. Dad will be making me a kite the way he did long ago, and flying it for me, too, or I will be in the kitchen in the afternoon after I have come back from school, Mum will make a cup of tea, and we will sit there yarning away about nothing in particular. But then come the nights when Joe Waters and I are fooling around with his bike and Dad comes up the road and saying, 'Home we go to our loving wife and mother and one more round in the heavyweight championship of the world.' Then everything that happened in those three days comes back to me. Sometimes, even though I don't care, I can't sleep, because this good memory of mine goes into action making me lie awake for hours and hours.

Then for days on end I get annoyed at God for putting one across on me the way he did. If I had been a big sinner, it would have been different. I was a baby like other babies, a little boy like other little boys, and I certainly didn't do any big wrong. That's what I have against God. Me so little and he God. That's why I call him a pain in the neck every so often, and once or twice I have taken communion and bitten the wafer right through with my teeth to try and hurt him.

A child should have plenty of sleep, I think, three meals a day, with a soft drink now and then in between if he feels like it, plenty of room to play about in, and a home that's a little like Christmas morning all the time. Toothache or a cut knee or something would be all right for a child, but not much more than that in the way of pain. Certainly he shouldn't have to worry about his parents, or about anything at all for that matter. Except a little about school, how fast he can run, or whether he is going to be any good at football, and such mental questions as how big the world really is, all the way around, and what is behind the sky.

I was thinking something along those lines as Sister Francis and I were walking that time. By the time we had got past the cowsheds and halfway up the hill beyond, she was so puffed that we had to sit on a log beside the lane. All that green grass, the convent itself looking so big, the animals and trees and all that kind of farm stuff—they were all spread out around us. Sister Francis patted her old face with a handkerchief, tossed off 'Oh dear me' a couple of times, and said that if I didn't mind she would say some silent prayers. I said it was all right by me, and away she went, while I sat there thinking of Mum and Dad, and why on earth I had ever wanted a bike. I didn't really cry. Then after a while Sister touched me on the head with her hand, making me jump as though I was being woken up.

'I suppose we should be getting back, Jimmy,' she said.

'I'm ready when you are.'

'Would you like to talk to me about anything? Anything about your mother?'

'No thanks,' I told her. 'It isn't necessary, thank you all the same. It's mince for lunch today, isn't it?'

'I beg your pardon.'

'It's mince today, isn't it?'

'I believe it is.'

'It's Thursday, that's how I know,' I said to her as she got up and wobbled back to the lane like a sick black hen. She always wobbles when she first gets up after sitting down for any time.

I went over beside her and took her hand in case it made her feel ashamed to have to ask me—she is really very shaky on her pins, is Sister Francis—and together we set off back to the convent.

'Jimmy Sullivan,' she said, peering down at me and not looking too happy. 'God makes little boys stronger than old women in more ways than one.'

'Yes, Sister,' I said. 'I certainly am very strong. You don't have to worry about me.'

And darn me, I did feel strong, too. I felt as though I could lick the whole world, and not give a darn. The feeling lasted for hours afterwards. And ever since then, even when I can't sleep because of this good memory of mine, I tell myself how strong I am, that nothing will ever really get me down.